THE
RING'S LIST

BY
JADE NICOLE-BRACKEN

Matador
9 Priory Business Park,
Wistow Road, Kibworth Beauchamp,
Leicestershire. LE8 0RX
Tel: 0116 279 2299
Email: books@troubador.co.uk
Web: www.troubador.co.uk/matador
Twitter: @matadorbooks

ISBN 978 1838590 109

British Library Cataloguing in Publication Data.
A catalogue record for this book is available from the British Library.

Printed and bound in Great Britain by 4edge Limited
Typeset in 10.5pt ITC Giovanni Std by Troubador Publishing Ltd, Leicester, UK

Matador is an imprint of Troubador Publishing Ltd

This novel is dedicated specifically to two of my four grandchildren, who gave me the initial inspiration to put pen to paper, and to my dad, who passed away in 2008.

The help and support of all my immediate family is herewith gratefully acknowledged.

Jade Nicole-Bracken is a pseudonym.

CHAPTER 1

25 January 1993

The clock struck one (the mouse ran down, hickory dickory dock... funny how the most childish of thoughts suddenly flash into one's mind for no apparent or logical reason at the most unexpected of times, he mused) as he stood in the cold, rain lashing down, his eyes fixed firmly on the church clock.

Just 30 minutes to go and the plan that he had been working on for so long could at last be implemented.

Just 30 minutes to go (no, perhaps 29 now) before ETA – decidedly quiet (perhaps too quiet), but he put that down to the appalling weather – however, you expect nothing less in January in this part of the world, and that it had been Burns Night into the bargain – so he assumed that most Scottish people had better things to do with their time indoors on such a foul night than loiter outside small parish churches anywhere north of the border (but particularly those in Leith, Lothian, Scortland).

At 37, Steven Martin Johns (Martin after his dad) would have described himself as a cheerful cynic now, when he should have been in his prime, he was just full of hate and revenge.

He was of average height (slightly less than six feet) and build (slightly more than 13 stone). His fitness could have been better but, considering his recent ordeals, it was passable.

However, he hoped that these past trials and tribulations would soon be over and 'the Plan' that he had been working on since 1979 would lead him to finally get some closure, thus being able to start life afresh.

Now only 25 minutes to go, but he was not getting any drier – he moved back into the shadows, collar up, and waited with as much patience as he could muster, chewing on yet another piece of his favourite gum.

PROLOGUE

He was of course not guilty, but the jury had not found him so and the judge had sent him down for 16 years.

He had seen one or two jails, but they had finally settled on Inverness for him (although he often wondered why it had to be so far away from home. However as he had no immediate family living nearby, apart from his Uncle Reg, so guessed it didn't really matter where he was put to serve his time).

His lawyer had not been brilliant but said that the case could go either way – in the end, however, the jury was unanimous and all his protestations fell on deaf ears; although his appeal was granted, the outcome was the same (although they did reduce the sentence slightly, to just under 13 years, for some strange and unknown reason).

That day (1 August 1979) will of course be one that he would never forget (and because he had always protested his innocence he had been incarcerated for almost the whole term) and so it happened to be Burns Night one year ago to the day (1992) when the doors of the Inverness City Prison were opened for him to walk free.

Steve had had a good job, but was without parents, and most of his elderly relatives had died when he was

3

young (except for dear old Uncle Reg) so at that particular moment in time (1000 hours GMT) he had little to his name in the way of belongings (several layers of clothes, mostly on, and the proverbial overnight bag).

Having walked to the station, he promptly found his rail ticket for the Caledonian overnight express to London waiting for him at the ticket office, and he whiled away the day (not bad, he thought, for the end of January, weather-wise, albeit cold) in and out of the waiting room and café, alternately drinking coffee and people watching.

Apart from the odd *helloo* and *cheerio now*, he spoke little, and as soon as he boarded the train he found his cabin and slept most of the way to the capital.

PROLOGUE

The month of September 1978 had started off like most other days.

Just turned 22 (single, no kids), he had set off on his 45-minute drive to work very early one Friday morning, not knowing that an unscheduled stop would change his life forever. Rounding a bend on the outskirts of his village home (Little Berkhamsted, Herts) on his way to work at Luton Airport, he came across a blue Toyota skewed across the road, door open and the driver half out of the car.

If only he had driven on but he stopped out of instinct and went to see if he could help – as he had done some first aid training in the recent past, he bent down to examine the body.

There was still life there so he instinctively tried to resuscitate him... and then the rest was a blur: they came from nowhere, cops everywhere (as though they had been lying in wait just for him!), and arrested him for attempted murder! What motive could there possibly be for him being culpable, or had it just been a case of being in the wrong place at the wrong time?

The only evidence was that he was there and had blood on his hands (from his first aid efforts, of course).

He never knew if the police really believed in the case or whether it was a frame-up instigated by person or persons unknown, but once they took the decision to prosecute on a murder charge (the victim passed away a few days later), they threw everything at him and against only the pleas of his lawyer he was convicted.

He had, of course, had plenty of time to think of a plan to find out who had framed him for murder that fateful September day, but obviously his first thoughts were of anger and revenge.

He thought of commissioning private detectives to look into things whilst he was doing his time but he didn't trust anyone anymore (except for his Uncle Reg).

The victim had been a 35-year-old banker named Jon Armstrong (a branch manager, not one of the now-disliked investment types). He lived in Herts with a wife and two kids, all standard stuff.

No other motive was ever found (which is why the cops probably thought, by process of elimination, that it must be him after some previous road rage incident or similar).

His theory had been that it was a clear case of mistaken identity or Armstrong was suspected to have involved himself (deliberately or accidentally) in a ring of crooks and there had been some sort of internal squabble and someone was trying to keep him from spilling his guts, as they say.

It appeared to him now more likely to be the latter but none of this came out at the trial, and owing to what he then thought was 'some bent copper' he was sent down.

He had gone over all the trial reports and newspaper reports, of course, ad nauseum, but nothing new had emerged. Then, just by chance, he had overheard that a guy called Adam Best from Herts, a long-time jailbird (in and out of jail over the years largely for pretty petty stuff), was due into Inverness Jail next week.

Maybe he had some local knowledge to share, but, before he had had a chance to fully talk to him, Steve was released. However, he decided that upon Adam's release he would be there to meet him...

CHAPTER 1A

Only five minutes to go now – Steve had, he thought, timed his trip to perfection.

In the last year he had joined one of those 'prison reform do-gooder organisations' (under an assumed name, of course).

He didn't stay long in London, just long enough to get in touch with his Uncle Reg, who had always believed in him and backed him to the hilt.

He had acted in his financial affairs prudently whilst Steve was being detained at Her Majesty's pleasure, and on his hunches quite a tidy sum on the old sharedealing front had been amassed.

Having joined 'Prisoners Reunited', Steve had decided to move north and found a nice little B&B in Leith, on the Firth of Forth, just outside Edinburgh, at a weekly rate of £100 (obviously not en suite).

He had been there for about nine months and hadn't been particularly looking forward to his first Scottish winter (weather-wise) as a free man, but all in all the locals were friendly enough and didn't pry into his past life too much.

He was known to his landlady et al as Colin Hoult.

It was about two and a half hours to Inverness (assuming the A9 was relatively clear of snow, ice and/ or fog) and, as he had been able to act as cover for his counterpart for northern Scotland when she was absent from work for holidays or sick leave etc., he had been able to make contact, without arising the suspicion of anyone, with her client there, one Adam Best.

Adam was older, in about his mid-fifties (but looked nearer retirement age, probably owing to his past life excesses).

He was one of those life and soul of the party types, always had something to say and an opinion on everything, but he had his darker side and no mistake.

Often surly, he would frequently start trouble and as a result was never considered for early release.

Following his visits, however, Steve had managed to build up an almost brotherly bond with him, convincing him that, even at his time of life, he could actually make a new life for himself outside of jail if only he was prepared to try hard enough.

Steve (or Colin Hoult, as Adam knew him to be) had therefore managed to discover, quite by accident, that the victim was known to Adam (both as his bank manager and as a colleague at the local snooker club).

For this reason alone, therefore, Steve had started to hatch 'the Plan' to discover who had been responsible for the murder of Jon Armstrong so that he could extract his revenge – and prove his innocence in the process.

PROLOGUE

Mortgage fraud has always occurred in the British property market – with so much money at stake there have always been crooks who have been prepared to risk professional disgrace to make their own fortune.

Some have no doubt never been caught and have gone on to live out their lives on the Spanish Costas with money to burn.

Others have been caught early on and been jailed, end of story.

The really clever ones, however, formed rings or cells, offering (anonymously, of course) targeted surveyors inducements to 'massage the figures' and so gain funds from a mortgage which was more than the property's open market value.

Once in, the surveyor is told to do more and more – they can't back out because threats are made to them and their families.

In times of high price rises, everyone's a winner (and the banks had, hitherto at any rate, been able to stand the losses), so often rings went undetected for years, and only the poor surveyor was left having sleepless nights (or worse).

The intermediaries were often financial advisors or legal conveyancing clerks, or just bent developers/investors.

The people at the top, however, could be from any walk of life, often living double lives to the extent that even their partners had no idea what was going on.

It appeared to Steve that Armstrong, in his blue Toyota, may have started to ask so many cutting questions about the surveyor's reputation (not to mention capability) that he had been got rid of.

But by whom? Was it a Ring or a one-off?

Steve had been unable to find out much more, so he was hoping Adam might be able to shed some light on his former bank manager and snooker-playing acquaintance.

CHAPTER 13

The church clock indicated that it was now 1.30am. He had decided not to go to Inverness to meet Adam but instead he had paid for Adam to catch the late train to Edinburgh.

Miraculously, the rain had stopped now, and he moved out from his sheltered spot to meet up with Adam.

Adam had been convinced of late that he was being watched so didn't want to meet openly outside the jail, which was why he had suggested he book for London but get off at Edinburgh and then find Colin at Leith's local church – his digs were only around the corner and he had a key which would enable them to get into his room unseen.

Apart from a few local drunks, the area around the church was deserted. Muttering a few choice *good evenings*, he circuited the church once, then twice – no sight or sign of him.

After ten minutes he rang the rail station enquiry office from a nearby public phone box, but there was of course no answer at that time of day (24/7 working had not been invented back in 1993, especially as far as our nationalised industries were concerned).

Cursing British Rail, he opened another packet of chewing gum, and waited.

The church clock struck two – 2am and still no Adam. The train must have arrived by now; where the devil was he?

Had he dropped off to sleep, the idiot, missed his stop and ended up on his way to London after all?

Soaking wet and freezing cold, he decided to drive to the station in his old Skoda estate car but as he turned the corner into Station Road he found… flashing blue lights, several policemen, an ambulance and a small group of people in the short stay car park.

He rushed over, only to find the casualty was already being taken to the waiting ambulance – the patient was Adam Best!

Momentarily, Steve couldn't move or speak. What had happened? Was it fate? An accident? Or had he been got at after all, as he had been fearing he would be of late? What should he do now?

Quickly gathering his thoughts, he mingled with the crowd. One said he would be taken to the main Queen Elizabeth Hospital, another said he saw a man run off after a fight and a third said he had just fallen down in a drunken stupor.

Steve decided to scarper, and drive back to his B&B, with a view to going to the hospital in the morning 'as his brother' to visit him.

The only trouble with that was: what if he died overnight, or was being watched?

If the former, so much for his Plan – cursing again, he eventually dropped off into an uneasy doze.

CHAPTER 2

Knock, knock… "Did you want breakfast this morning, Colin?"

He woke with a start to find his landlady's head poking round the door. "It's 9am, and you are usually up well before now for one of my Saturday morning fry-ups, aren't you?"

He muttered, "Yes please, I'll be down in a minute," and she withdrew. He had eaten and was in his car by 10am.

He was trembling now – should he wait until normal visiting hours? Would he have a police guard? Would it be possible to sneak in straight away?

He decided, somewhat reluctantly, that discretion was the better part of valour and went instead to enquire of the visiting times and was told 2pm.

Surprisingly, they gave him the ward details (B1) as well, which filled him with a bit more optimism that at least he wasn't under any police guard (and he hadn't died overnight!).

At 2pm he duly queued with the obligatory grapes and flowers and found Adam in a bed in the far corner.

"Adam," he said, "are you okay? What the devil happened last night?"

Adam looked pale and drawn, but smiled and then put a finger to his lips to indicate quiet.

After a few moments he said, in rather a loud voice, "Colin, so nice that you could come straight away. Had a bit of a fall last night but I'll be okay. You couldn't give me your shoulder to lean on, could you, so that I can get to the gents'? The nurses here are so busy, and I need to go now."

Once in the loos, however, he lowered his voice to a whisper. "I told you," he said, in a panicky voice so unlike him. "They are after me. I didn't fall, I was attacked. I need your help – you got me into this mess so I want out quick. You owe me." He glared, then seemed to visibly soften, as though he had got a big weight off his chest.

Steve took a deep breath and said, "Okay, but grant me one night at my place before you leave, and then we'll call it quits. No pressure but just one night: that's all I ask; if we can get you out from here early before anyone knows you've gone, then you can disappear the day after."

Adam glared at him again. "Why should I? I don't know you from Adam (excuse the pun!), do I? Why are you so interested in me of late, anyway?"

Steve stepped forward and whispered, "You know me as Colin Hoult but my real name is Steven Martin Johns, inside, wrongly, for 13 years for the attempted murder of your ex-bank manager and fellow snooker player from Hertfordshire, one Jon Armstrong."

Now it was Adam's turn to be dumbstruck, but having looked him up and down several times, said, "Well, I'll be blowed; yes, I remember that case now. Okay, then, I agree that I will leave with you tonight and leave Leith tomorrow

15

morning. So you will have a maximum of 14 hours, then I'm off."

If only he knew what was to befall him in the next 24 hours, he would probably have decided to depart straight away.

CHAPTER 2A

Evening visiting was busy and Adam wasn't too badly injured from his "fall" after all – they got back to the car and to Steven's B&B at about 8pm.

He put the telly on to hide any noise of their talking, said goodnight to his landlady by saying he was retiring to bed extra early that night, and then locked the door.

They sat opposite each other, hot coffees in hand, and started talking.

Colin (or Steve, as Adam now knew him to be) filled him in with some background information (on a need-to-know basis only), including the trial and what he had been doing since.

Adam listened intently and when he had finished sat quietly for a moment. Then he got up and with his back to the fire said, "That confirms it then. You are right, of course – it is highly likely that it is a case of mortgage fraud, possibly on a massive scale, and now 'the Ring' know you are out of jail…"

"But they don't know where I am," Steve interjected, "because I have changed my name."

"Possibly true," he conceded, "but they know me – because of my relationship with the murder victim, Jon Armstrong – he was my brother-in-law!"

They say it's a small world – Steve looked at him totally nonplussed.

Talk about the best laid plans of mice and men… but it could be a double-edged sword – what he had just said could open up big possibilities for him to finally solve the mystery which had been bugging him for years (but, on the other hand, it had now been brought home to him just how dangerous a venture he was rapidly becoming embroiled in).

He could of course stop and just disappear off into the sunset, but there again he would always be wondering who did it, whilst constantly looking over his shoulder in case they came after him as well.

No, he thought, he must carry on to uncover the truth, but appreciated Adam's predicament.

"So," he said, after a long pause, "what do you propose to do now?"

Adam frowned. "Why, get the hell out of here, of course. I still value my life too much, such as it is. If they know I am in touch with you they'll hang me out to dry before you can say Jack Robinson. Since your trial I strongly suspect that I have been 'watched' but left alone, then I was in jail when you were released one year ago, but as from now I suspect that I will be watched again. I have already been 'got at' once and if I don't get away soon they will be 'sending the boys round again'." He pointed to his injuries. "But this time to do a better job."

"Then why did you agree to help me?"

Adam looked at him with a slightly sympathetic smile. "Because of your help as part of the 'Prisoner's Reunited' scheme and partly because I think I know some of the people involved in 'the Ring'."

Steven's heart was racing now. "For God's sake, then, tell me, please."

Adam's whole demeanour changed at a stroke. "Ah, well, that depends on how big your chequebook is," he said. "Whether I tell you or not, I can't risk them finding out that we have ever met outside jail – there is the risk that they may already know, of course, in which case we are both dead men walking, make no mistake about that. Assuming they don't and I tell you then I am obviously at risk of being found out as 'the tell-tale who can't hold his waters' so, ditto, I'm still a dead man."

"How much do you want?" said Steve, almost reaching for his chequebook there and then.

"I have my price, but I don't know if you can afford it. I would want cash, obviously, enough to get out of Britain – always fancied Bulgaria, actually."

CHAPTER

Born just before the war (9 November 1937, actually) in Staffordshire, Adam Gregory Best grew up with his aunty and was a half-decent footballer in his day.

He had had trials with Derby County FC in the late 1950s but then booze and women took over.

He married in the mid-sixties to Armstrong's older sister, Joanne, but an early separation occurred and by 1970 he was doing odd builders' jobs for various locals.

He used to go to the local snooker club, which, unfortunately, his former brother-in-law also used to frequent (unfortunately because he hated Armstrong's guts because of his acrimonious divorce from his sister).

Jon Armstrong, on the other hand, was, at aged 30, at the top of his career, being the local branch manager for a major high street bank.

But then Adam went off the straight and narrow and ended up being jailed for burglary to fund his drug addiction (his latest stretch had been for 13 months).

Armstrong, though, had been born with a silver spoon in his mouth, went to uni and straight into banking, becoming a branch manager at the very, very young age of 29.

From then, however, all he could think about was retiring at 50 so that he could sit on the end of some Caribbean island pier, fishing, and smoking his favourite Cuban Havana cigars.

Steve was not a man to be messed with, but at the same time he abhorred violence. However he would not be blackmailed, but there again, if the end justified the means...

He thought quickly as he poured two single malts for them both, then said, "It depends how much of a cash sum you want now – I am barely earning enough to pay my way at the moment so I have little cash to draw on instantly and I assume that you still wish to leave first thing tomorrow, as planned, so that if you are still being watched you will not arouse undue suspicion because you will still arrive in the capital as planned, albeit a day late, which is reasonable considering the inclement weather."

He was in full flow now. "It may be that they are already onto you (whether you tell me owt or not) but maybe last night's 'attack' was just a coincidence – a drunken brawl – you know what Edinburgh's like on a Saturday night."

Steve took a deep breath. "I suggest that we never meet again after tonight, and I will pay you to get back on the train to London first thing tomorrow, plus £500 which I can get from the bank when they open at 9.30am tomorrow, on the basis that when you get to London you go to my uncle's house in Colchester for a further cash sum of £2,000 to get you out of the country etc. BUT you tell me all the names you know before you go."

He paused, then added, "It's down to whether we trust each other or not. If not then I don't get the list and you don't get the cash and still run the risk of being 'topped'. What's it to be, Adam?"

It was now 12.30 on the Monday morning – he could tell Adam was torn between asking for more, accepting the offer or cutting and running.

"Okay," said Adam, finally, "even though Jon was never my favourite relative, I guess I owe him that much and because of your recent friendship and help to me whilst in prison of late, I will agree to the following:

"One. You give me the down payment of £500 when the bank opens later this morning.

"Two. Get your uncle on the phone now so that I can confirm that he exists and so I can arrange a meeting place in London for me to receive the balance of £2,000.

"Three. You buy the train ticket for me tomorrow as well, and only then will I give you a written list of the names that I have."

They shook hands and sank back into their respective easy chairs, both visibly shattered.

CHAPTER

Steve never saw Adam again, but neither did Uncle Reg!

They implemented their agreement, including speaking to Uncle Reg – he was brilliant, cottoned on straight away, and Adam was happy to get on his way at 10am with the £500 and a ticket for the Smoke in his pocket.

However, as that day passed and then Tuesday the 28th, he never showed up at the pre-arranged meeting point in London.

As nothing of note had appeared on the news or in the nationals, Steve became apprehensive – presumably 'they' had got at him, and this time fatally.

What if he had talked and he was now being watched?

He didn't feel that he could go to Uncle Reg's as that would put his life in danger.

Left with no other option, he quickly packed, explained to his landlady that he had to leave suddenly, owing to a family bereavement (hoping as he spoke that he was not tempting providence!), got into his old Skoda Estate car and just drove.

The one plus that had come out of the last few days was of course that he now had a list of names.

Not much to go on, perhaps, but more than he had accumulated in the last umpteen years.

In the meantime, where to go as a base, and what about a job?

He had found himself driving south on the A1 on a cold and windy winter's morning.

He stopped for a break at McDonald's in the Blaydon area of Newcastle upon Tyne but quickly carried on and after about 250 miles in total found himself on the A1, some 160 miles or so from London.

During his second break from driving, his eyes fell on some travel information in the service station foyer, namely a rail map of England. He thought that it might be handy to be close to one of the East Coast Mainline railway stations – Doncaster was close by so he chose that.

CHAPTER

THE LIST.

There had been seven names listed by Adam (including Jon Armstrong, of course). He didn't know whether he expected more but hoped that "quality was going to prove to be better than quantity" (but guessed that only time would be the judge of that):

- Jon Armstrong, bank manager, of Potters Bar – now dead, of course!
- Robert Clarke, solicitor, of Essex t/a Goulding and Co.
- Philip White, also of Essex, surveyor and valuer – self-employed.
- Miss Penelope Banks, financial advisor, of Herts – also self-employed.
- Trevor Eagles, director of Southern Properties Ltd, registered office in Central London.
- Mrs Vanessa Downing, of Hertfordshire County Council.
- George Williamson MP.

How Adam had got to know all this he didn't know for sure (perhaps in part via Jon Armstrong at the snooker club) but what the hell – he couldn't give a monkey's as long as all the entries were genuine.

Armstrong was born in 1943 (a war baby); he was just 35 when he met his end. Brought up in Harpenden, he had gone to uni and risen quickly to become a branch manager, first in Ware and then in Welwyn Garden City. Living in Potters Bar, both his and Steve's respective drives to work were different (except for a mile or so on the B158) and it was on this stretch of B road where he had met his untimely end (and where Steve had found him and been framed for his murder).

He quickly ran down the list and noticed that there was a geographical connection to Essex and Hertfordshire (which was perhaps encouraging, or was it only coincidental?).

However, the last two names hit him like a brick, because he happened to know that the former was now the leader of the said county council and the latter was not only the local MP but also a government minister, namely the present secretary of state for the environment!

CHAPTER 4

In the morning, he thought he would make contact with Uncle Reg and buy a paper.

Reading the latter before he rang the former, he quickly learnt about Adam (apparently there had been a bit in the local rag as well, from what Uncle Reg subsequently told him).

It was put down as an accident (but to Steve it confirmed that the boys had caught up with him again).

So had he talked, and were they after him now as well?

It was a good job that he had moved from Leith, he thought, but so as to convince himself that he was 'untraceable' he decided to move further south, and settled upon a small town near the Derbyshire/Staffordshire border, albeit fairly close to East Midlands Airport – Uttoxeter.

Once in Uttoxeter, he contacted his Uncle Reg again, and asked if they could meet at some neutral venue – naturally he said yes straight away and they settled on the Watford Gap Service Station on the M1 the next day at 10.30am.

Steve had always liked (and had the utmost respect for) his uncle – he was his dad's younger brother by three years, both survivors of Dunkirk, but his dad had died in an industrial accident in 1966, when Steve was just ten, and accordingly had seen a lot of his uncle in his formative years.

Now in his early seventies, he was quite well off and very fit and active for his age. He had been prepared to help/back Steve from the beginning, presumably in memory of his older brother. There was a big risk, in Steve's opinion, that the Ring could easily trace and 'visit' his uncle, therefore he thought he had a duty to warn him of the risk, but at the same time wanted to ask him his opinion about how he might best move forward in general terms and specifically about 'the List'.

CHAPTER 4A

They were both on time and chose a quiet corner of the café on the southbound side.

Steve updated him on all the happenings since Burns Night, including the seven names on the list. Reg was quite dismissive of any risk to himself: "I have had my three score years and ten," he said in a matter-of-fact tone. "Look at your dad; I've lived over 25 years longer than him, thanks to his heroics towards me at Dunkirk in 1940, and 50 years longer than some of my war buddies therefrom.

"Remember, old soldiers never die; they simply fade away. I don't intend spending my last days lingering at death's door in some old people's home. I can handle myself, and everything I have is left to you, anyway, as I have no other family and you deserve it."

What he said didn't surprise Steve in the slightest, but nevertheless he expressed his love and gratitude for his uncle yet again.

Reg did agree, however, that he should stay away from Colchester for the foreseeable, thought Uttoxeter was okay for now and noted that East Midlands Airport was nearby and they were always looking for radio control staff so a job of some sort should be possible, even if it turned out to be part-time or on a shift basis to start with.

Steve said that he would look for somewhere to stay later that day, but time to look at 'the List's' names in a bit more detail now.

Being born and bred in Essex, Reg had heard of Goulding and Co. and said he would try to investigate Robert Clarke further.

He had not heard of Philip White but again said he would try and discover some basics about the man as soon as possible.

They discussed the private detective scenario again, but Steve decided against it – however, Reg agreed it looked like a big-time organised crime operation, and the Ring contained enough 'expertise' (at least on paper) to operate the mortgage fraud system (to include the leader of a county council and an MP it must be big) but of course nothing was proved yet and the list could be a total fabrication – after all, they only had Adam's word for any of this.

Steve wondered who had killed Jon Armstrong but Reg said it would have probably been some hired hitman (probably ditto for Adam as well – after all why should the ringleaders 'soil their hands' with such tasks when they could employ some 'low life' to do it for them?).

Armstrong had probably unwittingly uncovered some transaction which didn't look quite right but somehow it had alerted the Ring and they had silenced him quickly just in case.

They agreed to reconvene in one week's time – Steve agreed to look into the financial advisor, Miss P. Banks, and Southern Properties in the intervening time (not knowing, of course, that his research into the former would soon lead him all the way to Florida!).

CHAPTER 5

Back at their respective homes (Steve had booked into the Ship Inn for now), they started to do some research into the names on the list.

Reg got his computer going whilst Steve went down to the local library and made some block bookings to use their internet equipment.

T'internet (and the www) is more and more regarded as the Bible for making the world go round these days, but in those heady days of early IT development it was rather less so; certainly Steve and Reg still regarded any results obtained as going hand-in-hand with a large pinch of salt – could be useful in a very limited way but not the be all and end all, and, anyway, they often found that their computers crashed as soon as they got to an interesting bit!

Reg had done a lot of research like this before because he had been a forerunner in the field of genealogy and had built up quite an impressive family tree of the Johnses, dating back to circa 1740 (following many an hour in front of the microfiches and film readers at various archive libraries). Reginald Arthur Johns (born 7 January 1921) was of course included thereon.

The week passed quickly, and it was Saturday 8 February, now, but not much warmer, as he drove down the M1 again to the same service station (nice snowdrops, he thought, as he parked the car).

Once Reg arrived, they exchanged information they had each found to date.

Robert Hubert Clarke of Gouldings, Colchester, Essex. Now 60, part-time consultant, been with the firm man and boy (and was therefore 45 back in 1978), studied at the Bar etc. They discussed ways of trying to meet him and set up a bit of a 'sting'.

However, they needed to be careful not to avoid any suspicion whatsoever – Reg could go on pretext of making a new will or similar, but they are usually done by junior staff so that might not be a guaranteed way of meeting him anyway.

They passed on to others, making a mental note to come back to him at the end.

Philip White didn't seem to be around the area any more, but if still in his early fifties he was likely to be in employment somewhere doing something.

Reg was going to try and contact the RICS's HQ at Great George Street in London but hadn't made the time as yet. "He could have been got rid of by now, of course," said Reg in his concluding comments.

Steve had managed to discover some interesting facts about its principal director, Trevor Eagles – he had apparently died of a heart attack in 1988! (Had he been got rid of as well, they wondered?) But there was little to be gained by pursuing him or Southern Properties now, they thought.

On Penny Banks: nowt!

Do they pursue Downing and Williamson, they wondered? Vanessa Downing was an accountant, born 1928, and George Williamson was an economist, born 1926 – both Tories.

They mulled over further and then agreed to meet again in about two weeks' time.

CHAPTER 5A

Late February now (Friday the 21st) – the snowdrops had certainly been early this year (crocuses to follow, and then the daffs, he thought, as he waited for Reg in their usual seats) – seemed a lifetime away from Leith's foul winter weather.

Little more had been found out in the interim period by either of them, so Reg decided to take the bull by the horns. "I suggest," he said, "that I try and visit Jon Armstrong's widow."

Steve was dumbstruck – why hadn't he thought of that himself? – but, as Reg pointed out, he couldn't go in case she recognised him from the court case, whereas Reg would be less conspicuous.

After a while, Steve reluctantly agreed; they didn't make another time to meet up – just left Reg to make contact with Steve once he had met her.

After Steve left, Reg returned to his seat with another coffee, and sat for at least half an hour, deep in thought. "Vanessa Downing, eh? Now there's a blast from the past – I could soon be between a 'rock and a hard place' in all of this but, what the hell, family comes first, and anyway, I owe it to his dad to help Steve, whatever the personal sacrifice to me."

As he got up to leave, he felt (and probably looked) at least ten years older.

CHAPTER 6

It appeared that Mrs Armstrong had stayed in Potters Bar after 1 September 1978, but had moved from the matrimonial home to a first-floor flat. Born in 1948, her two kids had long since left home.

Her apartment looked nice enough from the outside, if not over ostentatious.

Reg's problem had been how to get to speak to her initially – any 'accidentally on purpose' chance meeting was likely to take a while to set up, and Reg didn't feel there was that time to play with, so he thought he would just 'take the bull by the horns' and broach the subject with her directly by using Jon's brother-in-law (Adam Best) as an opening gambit.

He had found her phone number via Directory Enquiries and rang her up – at the second attempt he got through.

He pretended to be a private detective, client confidential at this stage, investigating 'past misdemeanours' at the bank, but being aware of Jon's untimely death.

She was really taken aback after all this time about receiving such a call, but did eventually agree to meet him this coming Saturday. So it was 1 March when he arrived at her flat. When was the last time I wore a tie? he thought, as he locked the car and strode purposefully over to the front door. She let him in and he sat down, but she didn't offer him a drink.

He explained his call in a bit more detail, and asked about her deceased husband's career with the bank.

She confirmed his rapid rise up the banking ladder, but he noted how 'distant' she seemed to be about him (perhaps time had healed the scars somewhat).

Nothing she said seemed to give him any particular lead, so he took a slightly different tack and mentioned one or two people on the list – still nothing – but as soon as he mentioned Penny Banks she just blew up into a rage and demanded he leave.

Blown it now, good and proper, he thought, but just as he got to the door she said, "Wait, please, I need to tell somebody after all these years." Sobbing uncontrollably, she managed to blurt out, "Ms Penelope Banks was the reason my husband died…"

CHAPTER 6A

He made her a cup of black tea – glancing at her from the kitchen/diner, he realised that she was not unattractive, and wondered what had happened to cause the marriage to fail. Grass is always greener on the other side probably, although the fault is rarely just one way in these cases, he reckoned.

However, when one gets all material things so early in life, happiness rarely follows, and he had probably started to go off the straight and narrow with business meetings turning to rounds of golf, lunches, conferences away from home, clandestine meetings etc.

But would she decide to confide in him now or just clam up?

He sat down – she said thanks, mumbled an apology and then appeared to pull herself together a bit and said, "What do you know about that slut Banks then?"

He managed to disguise his shock at the reference to her 'that slut' description, but said that she wasn't a client of his and thought that she may have been involved in dealings with his client at the bank – professionally, of course: maybe as an independent financial advisor.

"Professionally? You must be joking – she was the slut that had an affair with my husband, fleeced him of half of his fortune and then within a week of his death disappeared across the pond – Florida I believe…"

Reg had always been good at hiding his emotions, but on this occasion even he could not conceal his amazement at her latest revelations.

He quickly reassessed the situation – was Banks's name on Adam's list because of her involvement with 'the Ring' or just because she had been with Jon for personal reasons? Should he divulge to her more of what he knew of the Ring and the suspected mortgage fraud activities etc., or play it cool and just concentrate on pumping her about Banks's apparent relationship with her husband, and then leave?

Time, he thought, for some white lies.

CHAPTER 6B

"Could I ask you," he said, "why if, as you say, she had been the reason for your husband dying, did you let her get away with it? In other words, why didn't you tell the police rather than stand by and let someone else take the rap?"

"How do you know I didn't?" she retorted – she tensed again, and he immediately wondered if he had gone too far after all. "Who are you anyway? I'm starting to suspect that you have come here under false pretences. I only have to press this buzzer here –" she pointed to it on the wall next to where she was sitting "– and the cops will come running."

Okay, he said to himself, here goes, shit or bust... "Because, Mrs Armstrong, as I have already said, I am here representing a client of mine. I am here about the bank side of things, in a way, but I admit that I am not a private detective, as such."

He took a deep breath, tented his fingers, and then spoke again. "I am here to find out more about your husband's death, and I can reliably inform you that, whilst Jon's killing could have been organised by Banks, my suspicions (based on facts that I have recently obtained from my nephew) are that he was murdered for far more sinister reasons."

He paused and she stared at him, somewhat nonplussed – he noted that she had taken her finger off the buzzer now.

"What the devil are you talking about?" she croaked.

"How do you know that Banks was definitely involved?" said Reg. "What was her motive?"

"I would have thought that was obvious," she snapped back. "Because he had confessed to me and we wanted to make a fresh start – hell hath no fury like a woman scorned and all that."

"That's as may be," said Reg. "Obviously I didn't know that. BUT I still think Jon's murder was for other reasons, which I will come to in a minute, but, cards on the table, whoever killed Jon got away with it and it is for this reason that my trail has led me to Banks, and then you.

"If I don't know anything else about this matter, I definitely know this to be correct because I know that the person wrongly convicted was my nephew, Steven Johns, so we are both united in our determination to uncover the truth and get the full justice that he deserves."

"How do you know that the hitman was not acting for Penny though?" said Mrs Armstrong (or Christine, as Reg now knew her to be).

An hour had passed since Reg's announcement about his nephew having been wrongly incarcerated for her husband's murder. In that time, Reg had told her more than he was planning to about 'the Ring', mortgage fraud, Adam's list etc. (he didn't know why – perhaps he felt that it was time he found someone to talk to to get things off his chest as well).

"I guess the only way to know for certain," Reg said, "is to find out the truth, and my intentions are, from what you have been telling me over the last hour or so, to try and trace Penny Banks and ask her. So, do you know where she went exactly and where she is now? And, perhaps more importantly, do you wish to become involved in our search for the truth, even to the extent of meeting my nephew and/or making the journey to – Florida did you say? – with one or both of us."

CHAPTER 7

Before he got back to the car, he rang Steve, but there was no answer – probably still at the library, he thought, or work. He got a bite to eat and mused over the meeting he had just had. He concluded that it could be very risky, but matters really did need sorting out now once and for all.

Having driven home, he rang again, and this time Steve answered.

Reg imparted what had happened at his meeting – Steve was overjoyed at a breakthrough at last, but Reg tempered his enthusiasm by suggesting that, just because a link appeared to have been established, finding her would be an altogether different matter.

But, more importantly, perhaps, who was to be tasked with going to Florida?

Steve thought that the time was right for him to meet Christine (mainly because she had decided that she wanted in so as to take an active role in finding Penny, not just be a sleeping partner, so to speak).

Reg, however, thought that the need-to-know principle was a better way forward so that, if the Ring cottoned on that they were investigating matters, there were 'enough breaks in the chain' to make it more difficult for them to be traced.

At present, Reg was the least at risk, then Steve and finally Christine. Christine could hardly go on her own. Reg offered but Steve would not hear of it.

He thought that if only one was going it should be him – Reg was better at the research side of things anyway, and Steve was itching to get stuck into something tangible.

They eventually agreed that, if one, it would be Steve and, if two, it would be Steve and Christine as partners.

If Reg then found out some other leads, he could always phone these through and anyway Christine said she would pay so if she insisted on coming they could hardly say no.

Reluctantly, Reg felt he had to agree, but wondered just what a big misjudgement this would turn out to be in the final analysis.

Having been involved in the aviation industry for some years, Steve had a few contacts scattered around the country.

He put some feelers out and within ten days bits of info started to drip feed back to him.

Then, out of the blue, an acquaintance at Gatwick (previously Manchester) rang him on 16 March to say that if he went to the Gulf Coast of Florida and headed for Naples, he might find a Ms P. Banks working as (surprise, surprise) a financial advisor and real estate operative!

On Saturday 20 March 1993, Steve and Christine boarded a Virgin B747 jumbo jet at Gatwick bound for Miami.

CHAPTER 7A

Steve and Chris (she preferred the shortened form when amongst friends) had met for the first time the previous week.

Steve had never really been a womaniser – one or two casual relationships in his late teens but obviously for over 14 years plus he had been incommunicado from all that sort of thing.

Chris had also stayed single (if not completely celibate).

They had booked a package holiday, on a two-room basis, at the Gulf Coast Motel in Naples, and a car (with automatic transmission, of course).

Their plan was simple enough – first check out whether the info he had been given from his former work colleague was correct and then maybe create a bit of a sting so that the extent of Penny's involvement in Jon's death could be determined beyond reasonable doubt. However, any question of force was quickly ruled out; the Yanks were pretty likely to come down heavily on foreigners (albeit English) parachuting in to become vigilantes.

The options of course were: no involvement, involvement in relation to the affair only, or involvement to do with 'the Ring'. The difficult bit of course was how to trick her into some sort of admission without giving away their true identities.

However, 15 years was a long time and with a beard/moustache Steve looked quite different from the fresh-faced 22-year-old that Penny might have remembered at the trial.

It was, however, agreed to be too risky for Chris to meet her directly at the same time, so she suggested that Steve be the one to meet her (on the pretence of wanting to invest in a holiday home to let out somewhere in the Naples area).

The flight was uneventful, as was the drive along the Tamiami Trail (Highway 41) west to Naples.

As soon as they had landed (neither had been there before) it was something of an understatement to say that it was simply the best place they had ever seen or been to by far. By the time they got to Naples they both felt that they were on holiday rather than on a journey of the utmost seriousness.

Steve in particular had never felt so good in a long, long time and as his head hit the pillow he wondered if he had fallen head over heels in love (with both Florida and Chris).

Back home, Reg at that very minute was thinking about the latter in very much the same way!

CHAPTER

On the Monday morning, still recovering from jetlag, they managed to find Penny's offices easily enough.

She was indeed working at a small branch office in the centre of Naples as both an independent financial advisor and an accompanied viewer.

Steve entered the office on spec (on the pretext of window shopping for a property to buy as both a holiday home and a partial let-out).

It had rained over night and he thought that it was going to be very humid (he was already sweating cobs and it was only 10am local time).

Before they had set off, Chris had tried to ring Reg from their motel to let him know how things were progressing but there had been no answer.

Penny was very helpful and he agreed to meet her for two viewings that very afternoon.

She appeared to have a ring on her wedding finger, but her name badge clearly said Miss P. Banks.

Now in her fortieth year, she was definitely an eye-catcher – long hair and legs, and green eyes; dressed to kill, you might say.

She seemed efficient enough, but Steve had a funny

feeling about her in as much as she was always talking at him rather than to him, and was always averting her gaze and never really looked him in the eyes the whole time he was in her office.

The office was plush but small, and there was only one other worker present; no other punter came in whilst he was there.

Having grabbed a quick bite to eat at one of the many fast food outlets nearby (a Perkins restaurant, as he recalled) he met her at 2pm at the first property and appeared interested as she treated him to the usual sales spiel.

He started to fish for some information. "So," he said, in as casual a manner as he could muster, "how long have you been here in Florida doing this job? If I may say, you don't sound 100 per cent American."

"Oh, quite a while," she replied, presumably wanting to give the impression that she knew her stuff and wasn't wet behind the ears. "I came over here over ten years ago, and liked it so much I decided to stay on."

"Yes, I like it too from what I have seen so far – so whereabouts do you hail from? I'm from the Home Counties but am working out of the Midlands at the moment."

She suddenly looked at him intently. "Do I know you?" she said.

He looked back and stated that he couldn't see how unless… his heart missed a beat… she too was from the Home Counties?

She didn't answer, as her mobile phone rang at that moment (saved by the bell, he thought) and when she

47

had finished she seemed to have forgotten what they were saying, so he quickly returned to the business in hand in order to try and divert attention away from her having any more recognition thoughts.

At the end of the second viewing, however, she returned to the earlier discussion of her own accord by stating that she had worked in the Home Counties for a spell but had not returned since 1981 and had no desire to do so in the future.

"But did you work in the same line of business back home?" Steve asked (he was determined to continue to probe into her past even if that risked her further suspicions).

"I did briefly, yes," she said, "more as just a financial advisor-cum-secretary but fancied a change after things didn't work out." She looked at him quickly. "Professionally, I mean," she added.

"Of course," Steve said, and moved swiftly on by arranging to call into the office in a couple of days' time, once he had given some reflective consideration to the pros and cons of the two properties he had just seen.

CHAPTER

That evening, early, Steve and Christine ate out, and he relayed how the day had gone.

They agreed it was inconclusive at present, but if she was telling the truth they both felt that her inclusion on Adam's list was warranted.

It amazed Steve how Chris appeared to have mellowed since they landed in Florida; she said she had found it very surprising too, but was nevertheless still determined to sort out what had actually happened in the lead-up to 1 September 1978 (as of course was he, but for somewhat different reasons).

They rang Reg whilst they were in the restaurant – he expressed caution about being too pushy with Penny; said he was fine but had not had too much luck at uncovering any more info and as a result was considering concentrating on Philip White by approaching the RICS direct.

Steve concurred, and said that they would probably have a drive down the coast to Marco Island tomorrow (ie a bit of a day off) before he re-met up with Penny. Christine had a quick chat with him and then they rang off to turn in for the night.

After they had hung up, Reg definitely made a mental note to ring up Robert Hubert Clarke in the very near future.

CHAPTER

They had had a lovely day at Marco Island, and Steve was at Penny's office at 9am on the Wednesday morning.

At the last minute, Chris had decided to come with him, but hover nearby (she wanted at least to 'see the cow', as she put it, even if she couldn't actually meet her – yet).

However, when the office opened, Penny wasn't there – the employee who was introduced himself as the manager, Martin Tyler (early thirties, tall with long blond hair in a pony tail, and very self-assured).

Steve introduced himself and explained the reason for his call. Martin said he was expecting Penny in any minute, and offered him an espresso whilst he waited.

After 20 minutes, Martin returned, and seemed a bit flustered.

"She should be in by now," he said. "It isn't her day off until tomorrow, and she went to do a viewing late yesterday, so I'd assumed that she went straight home from there." He checked the office diary. "Yes, here it is – a villa up towards Fort Myers, north of here."

He rang her and there was no answer but then the office phone rang; he picked up but when he finished he had gone a deathly white.

"What's the matter, Mr Tyler?" said Steve. "Was that her; is she poorly or something?"

Martin whispered, "I don't know. No, that wasn't her; it was the person she was due to meet last night. Apparently he showed up, but she didn't!"

Steve's brain went into overdrive in an instant.

He immediately began to have the unthinkable nightmare – that lightning had struck twice, ie Penny had been got rid of, and before too long he would be stuck with a second murder charge round his neck, but this time no prison sentence but the electric chair!

Had he got a cast-iron alibi this time (even though he had been with Chris for most of yesterday)?

He concluded that he hadn't, so he also concluded that he could well be "up shit creek without a paddle" – Reg, and Chris had warned him to be careful, but no: typical "gung ho" – in at the deep end and no apparent way of climbing out of the mire.

His mind cleared. "Perhaps she is at home," he said, "having been taken ill last night, or something."

Martin was silent, then said, "Possibly, but I think that is unlikely – she would have rung me if that was the case I'm sure. Although we work together, and see each other most nights, last night we didn't because it was my late night at the office. We don't live together, yet... we were due to move in together next week, as we are lovers."

CHAPTER 9A

He then got up and closed the shop by drawing down the blinds and locking the door.

From the car outside, Chris noticed this and immediately became fully alert – she went to get out of the car, but then checked herself and decided to observe a little longer.

Steve said nothing – he sensed that he was on a knife edge between finding out more (about Penny and/or the Ring) OR being the prime suspect if Martin decided to phone the police.

He could see that Martin was trying to decide how best to proceed.

He suddenly looked at Steve. "I'm not sure what to do, Mr Johns. I'd dash over to her house to check, but I'm expecting a very important business call from England any minute, and if I'm not here then my franchise business will be put at risk. You met her on Monday, didn't you – how was she then?"

Steve explained that he had only met her that one time, so had nothing to compare it to. However, she was okay professionally, and very thorough. "I'm sure you'll find everything's fine," he ended. Then, almost as an afterthought, said, "Do you want me to do anything to help, ie either go to her house to check or take the call that you are expecting?"

"Would you? Well, that's very kind of you." Then he hesitated. "But I don't know you, do I? How can I ask that of you? But there again I can't be in two places at once, can I… I don't know…" he tailed off, as if in a real quandary.

As he hadn't mentioned going to the police, Steve felt a bit more confident about things now.

"Mr Tyler, I appreciate that we have only just met but I hail from Herts, and understand Penny did too. I think you can say that English/American relations are pretty good at present, and, although I only came here this morning to follow up on the possibility of buying a house to rent out, I am happy to stand in for you if you prefer to go to Penny's house yourself (as a favour to my American cousins, so to speak). Furthermore, my partner is outside shopping, so alternatively we can both go check on her whilst you stay here if you prefer that. If needs be, you can then go there after your call, can't you (or not, as the case may be)?"

"Okay," he said, "time for a management decision, I guess – here's the address, and directions, and my phone number – about one hour all in should do it; if you both could go, and if needs be I can go at lunch time (or earlier if you find something 'negative') once I have spoken to my boss at Southern Properties, Mr White."

CHAPTER

One week had elapsed since his visit/meeting with Martin Tyler on 25 March.

It was therefore now the 1 April but so much had happened in that time that it felt more like one year than one week.

However, he remembered Martin's final words as clearly as if they had been spoken one minute ago: "Having spoken to my boss in London, Mr White of Southern Properties..."

To say that things had happened at a frenetic pace since Martin had uttered those last telling words was, to say the least, just about the understatement of the decade.

He had just about managed to disguise the massive shock of what he had just heard – all he could think about was the list that Adam Best had given him in Leith that January night.

Since then he had discovered that one had died (Trevor Eagles) and more recently another had disappeared (Adam Best) and now probably Penny Banks as well (albeit yet to be confirmed but likely that she was involved in 'the Ring' as well, ie not just as Jon Armstrong's lover).

However, he had managed to utter a controlled "See you later then", put the directions in his pocket and rushed off.

Finding Chris almost on the doorstep, he half ran, half pushed her into the car and drove off at high speed whilst filling her in on what had happened.

She too was flabbergasted, and wondered if they should go to Penny Banks's home or just head straight for the airport and back to England.

She was not cut out for this sort of thing, and realised just how dangerous a situation they had created for themselves.

Steve admitted that he had considered this as well, but on balance realised that, if they did rush home now, suspicion would automatically fall on them IF something had happened to Penny. Either way – they would soon know, presumably – he thought they should at least go see, and, depending on what they found, either go back to Martin or just ring him or, as a last resort, head to the airport for a quick getaway.

He was satisfied that Martin had nowt to do with the Ring, and Chris concurred, reluctantly, that Penny was (or perhaps more accurately had been whilst in England) involved in the Ring and therefore her relationship with her husband had been extra involvement on the side – but had her husband been involved in the Ring as well, and for some reason been got rid of?

She didn't know whether this reason was better than the other purely sexual possibility that she had assumed for so long was the one and only cause and nothing else was ever a possibility, but there was time for that to fully sink in in due course.

In the meantime, they both wished that they could speak to Adam for just five minutes to ask how he had been able to provide such an accurate list.

They also wished they could ring Reg to ask what he thought they should do now.

They got lost twice so it was nearly an hour since they had left Martin's office before they pulled up outside – all seemed quiet.

They rang the bell, then tried the door – it was locked. Round the back, however, a door was ajar – they called out then looked at each other in silence.

As if telepathically, they moved inside together (being careful not to touch anything).

What they found stopped them in their tracks.

CHAPTER 10A

The house had obviously been trashed – a radio sounded somewhere from an upstairs room but otherwise there was complete silence.

Moving carefully through the strewn contents, Steve called out, "Hello, is anybody there? Miss Banks..." and almost immediately they heard groaning sounds coming from the next room. Pushing the door fully open, they found her slumped on a settee, in a house coat which barely covered her lower body.

She looked in a bad way – Chris went forward, but Steve stayed back in the shadows of the doorway (he had been in this situation before and wasn't going to make the same mistake again!).

Penny opened her eyes and groaned again: "Oh, my back," she whimpered. "I can't feel my legs – I can't move – please help me."

"What happened, dear?" said Chris, stooping closer.

"I assume a robbery that went wrong. I was here yesterday tea time watching the early evening news on the TV before I set off for an evening viewing I had booked in up near Fort Myers when someone burst in and attacked me. I've been here ever since; don't know if they've taken much."

"Don't worry about that now; first things first. If it's your back, don't move and I'll ring for an ambulance to come and…" Then the back door burst open and a masked gunman appeared, brandishing a sawn-off shotgun.

He of course saw the two girls and raised his gun to shoot.

"I had a funny feeling that I had not completed the job," he drawled. "This will teach you to mess with Messrs White and…" Steve didn't wait any longer (although he realised in that split-second, as he struck down with all his force on the back of the intruder's neck, how interesting it would have been to have let him first finish his sentence before acting as he did, but was fully committed to his offensive action and couldn't have stopped in mid stroke, so to speak, even if he had wanted to).

The gunman swung round, his gun going off in the process, shattering the ceiling rose above their heads.

Steve then kicked him in the crown jewels and, as he doubled over, stamped down on his back, spread-eagling him on the carpet.

He had never handled a gun of any sort before, but nevertheless picked up the shotgun and held it to the gunman's head whilst snarling, "Don't move a muscle, pal, or you'll get both barrels."

He looked at Chris. "See if you can find something to tie him up with whilst he is still semi-conscious. Then we'll call the police as well as an ambulance."

He was feeling rather pleased with himself (albeit in an almost obscenely violent sort of way) as Chris came back after a few moments with what appeared to be a washing line and some small laundry items to gag him with.

58

All was quiet from the settee; presumably Penny had fainted.

They had just finished securing him when he began to come round.

"Who sent you here, scumbag?" said Steve, and raised the gun to his head again; however, it was obvious that he was not going to talk, so Chris went without further ado to ring for the emergency services.

At that very minute, Reg was putting the phone down having tried, yet again unsuccessfully, to speak to Robert H. Clarke.

CHAPTER 10B

In the next few moments, Penny started to stir.

As soon as she opened her eyes, she seemed to recognise Chris (and at the same time the penny seemed to drop as to who Steve was).

As if reading her mind, Chris said, "No; as you can see –" pointing to the gunman "– your attack had nowt to do with us, but I suspect he was sent to silence you before you had a chance to tell us anything about your relationship with my husband back in 1977/8 (but probably more importantly your work involving either Southern Properties and/or Philip White and/or Trevor Eagles).

"We –" pointing to Steve "– are both here from England to find out from you who was behind my husband's death, which Steve here was framed for—"

"I am Steve, by the way," interjected Steve, by way of introduction.

"—not to harm you," continued Chris, "although I am sorely tempted."

"Can you tell us anything at all, PLEASE?" added Steve. "Do you know him?" He pointed to the now-tied-up gunman.

She seemed to stare into space for what seemed an eternity (she knew she had seen him at their first meeting but just couldn't place him – however, 15 years is a long time and he does look somewhat different to how I remember him, she thought).

Then she said, "Who sent you here then? All this seems too much of a coincidence to me." Then, as an afterthought, said, "No, I don't know him," pointing to the gunman.

Steve explained his visit to her office that morning, as arranged, and the fact that Martin had sent them. "Because he was worried about you, but had to stay in the office to receive a phone call from Philip White of Southern Properties," he ended.

The emergency services sirens could be heard in the distance. "Quickly now, dear, none of us have got much time; just answer yes or no," said Steve.

She paused momentarily, then winced as she tried to change her position. "Yes, I was in love with Jon and, yes, I did get some of his money for myself, but I had no involvement with his death, I assure you. I acted as an independent financial advisor, and dealt with Jon's bank (that's how we met) but if you expect me to admit anything more (despite the attentions of our 'mutual friend' over there and despite your timely interventions of a few moments ago) you are sadly mistaken – as far as I am concerned, it's been a robbery gone horribly wrong, and that's all I'll say to the sheriff when he arrives. I'll not implicate either of you in my attack but by the same token don't pursue me regarding anything that happened in England in 1977/8 in my job, because quite simply I was only 'an Indian and not a chief' and was only doing as I was told – ie learning the ropes – and therefore I had nothing to do with any illicit mortgage fraud ring."

"Who said anything about a mortgage fraud ring?" said Steve. There was a deathly silence.

Because of the recent attack on her and all that she had just said, he didn't believe a word that she had just uttered – then the emergency services arrived.

CHAPTER 11

To cut a long story short, all four of them were carted off to the sheriff's office and hospital, respectively.

However, within 24 hours, Steve and Chris had been questioned separately and then released (presumably because their stories matched and because Penny had been true to her word and said it was a robbery that had gone wrong).

Their story had presumably been backed up by Martin as well, and the intruder had probably kept his mouth shut, so the cops had no reason to suspect or detain them further; on the contrary, they were hailed as heroes for what they had done to help Penny and detain the intruder with reasonable force.

Martin was also very grateful, but the trouble was that Penny was likely to be wheelchair-bound for the rest of her natural life (unlikely that she would be having any other affairs again, thought Chris). However, the intruder would be sent to jail for a long time, if that was any consolation.

They had spoken to Reg on the Friday, first thing, and Steve was really surprised by how critical Reg had been over what the two of them had done.

"You could quite easily have got yourself killed, never mind Chris," he said. "You need to get back home quickly where I can 'look after' you – you've found out what you can about Penny, and if Martin is 'clean' why stay out there any longer anyway? I suggest you quit whilst you are ahead."

Chris agreed, but Steve said he would have to think about it. "But as a place to live I much prefer where I am now than back home – weather-wise, if nothing else."

However, after a further few minutes of verbal, and sometimes rather heated exchanges, he agreed to book a return flight in the next couple of days.

CHAPTER 11A

In the meantime, he thought he would go and see Martin again (although he didn't tell Reg about that) and in the finish Chris didn't want to go with him so it was dinner time on 1 April when he walked into the office to find him on the phone.

His eyes lit up when he saw him, motioned him to take a seat, and quickly concluded his call. Then he walked up and shook his hand as though it was going to come off.

"I can't thank you enough for what you did last week at Penny's house," he said. "I just don't know what I would have done in that situation."

Steve said that he was sure that he would have managed – perhaps it was that there had been two of us that had made the difference.

Then he added, "How is Penny?"

"Could be worse – ie dead – but all in all she's just so grateful to be alive even though she realises that she may never walk again."

"Yes, I'm so sorry about that; she seems like a good kid, and all as a result of a robbery, eh?" Steve made the last statement as more of a question, but it didn't seem to register with Martin, who carried on heaping praise on him and Chris for what they had done to such an extent that it started to get a tad embarrassing.

"I just hope the phone call with Mr... White, was it...? was worth waiting for," said Steve.

This time he got a response. "Oh, he rang alright; waste of bloody time though – pardon my French but he makes my life a damn misery sometimes; that's bosses for you, I guess. In the end it was nothing mega after all, but he always rings twice a week, regular as clockwork, to keep tabs on his business operations out here in the US."

"I see," said Steve coolly (whilst rapidly thinking on his feet as to what he should say next – he really felt that MT had no idea at all what had been going on in his business franchise over the years, ie it was the Ring's way of laundering a large part of the money that they had accumulated over time, and Martin was just a front/cover for doing this). "I know what you mean – I had a boss like that once. How long have you been here, then? Penny said she has been over here for more than ten years, but I assume that you have always lived here."

"Hell yeah, 100 per cent Yank, me," said Martin proudly. "However, I have only been here in this office for five years – I found that I was quite good at selling, and was always interested in property (always envied Walt Disney for the way he shrewdly bought up vast areas of Florida swamp (incognito) for a pittance in order to bring his grand Disney World plans to fruition) so when this job came up I applied for it and got it. Penny joined me soon afterwards and, as they say, the rest is history."

"Anyway," said Steve, "I just popped round to let you know that I am off back home the day after tomorrow – I know I came here to buy a house in Florida, but recent events have put Chris off a bit, so we have decided to put it on hold for the moment. Obviously, give our regards to Penny, and if we change our minds we will certainly get back in touch with you."

Martin looked at him. "That's a shame," he said, "but I understand your decision completely. However, whilst I know nothing about Mr White's activities in England, Steve, should you wish to invest in the English property market, I could put a good word in for you – or, better still, you can ask him yourself if you like because he is due to land at Fort Myers Airport this afternoon."

CHAPTER 11B

Now what the —— does one do? he asked himself.

He had no doubt that Philip White was coming out (or had been sent out) to 'deal with him' himself – presumably because he was close to uncovering the truth.

Reg was right, of course: he should have left by now (or not even come at all).

Then he had an idea (must have come to him from all those years of thinking time he had had in Inverness Jail), so he said, "Thanks again, Martin, but I would not wish to do that at this stage (at least not directly). What I mean is that I would prefer an intermediary (a la the Walt Disney scenario that you were referring to earlier – albeit on a much smaller scale, of course). I am happy that that person be you if you think that it would not compromise you at all – I am obviously not asking you to do anything illegal, of course –" he thought as he said it just how ironic that last statement was in all the circumstances – "but you may fancy 'getting one over' on him given what we were saying earlier about 'bosses being pains' etc."

Martin didn't hesitate. "I guess I can find a way of doing that," he smiled, and they instinctively shook hands. "Just one condition, though: you don't tell Chris and I don't tell

Penny – the less they know now, the fewer lies they may be called upon to make up in the future."

Steve readily agreed, and they shook hands again.

"Shall we move into my private office," said Martin, "in case we wish to talk further before I go and collect him from the airport?"

As they walked across the room, Steve made a mental note to not only not tell Chris but to keep it quiet from Uncle Reg as well.

CHAPTER 12

Ever since the Watford Gap Service Station meeting with Steve at the end of February, Reg had been mulling over what to do next, and more importantly how to do it.

He admitted to himself that things had really started to change since the 1 March.

At 72, Reg was just under 30 years her senior, but since he had first set eyes on her his whole world had been turned upside down.

Why he suggested to Steve in late February that he should go and see her to find out more he just did not know (just curiosity, he guessed, to find out how much she really did know about 'the Ring').

That had probably backfired somewhat, as he would have given his right arm to go to Florida with her and had hardly been able to concentrate on much at all since.

He had never seen her in 1978 (except via poor-quality newspaper photographs) because he was abroad working on an important long fixed-term contract.

Therefore, not only did he never go to the trial but was away at the time of the incident as well, and when he returned Steve had been banged up.

It had taken Reg a long time to get over what had happened to his beloved nephew (he had had no kids himself – none that he knew of, anyway!), but he had vowed to himself to help Steve in whatever way he possibly could, once released.

Then he had met Chris – he hoped that she would be okay over in the States – but she had this notion that she wanted to gain her personal revenge on Penny (for her ex-husband's sake, he guessed), whereas 'the Ring' was an altogether different kettle of fish.

However, she would probably hear only what she wanted to hear, ie Jon and Penny's gory details, and little else.

He had kept his word about investigating Clarke and White, but his heart was not really in it anymore, and, despite what he told Steve, underneath it all he was really trying to dissuade him of taking further action in case he got caught up in the crossfire – even to the extent of telling him off the other day, for God's sake!

Now, owing to Chris's involvement, he was in a real quandary.

Last month he had promised Steve that he would ring up Robert Clarke; following their subsequent chat/near argument he had had with Steve he knew he could sit on the fence no longer but, fingers crossed, he was just waiting for them to return home in one piece (especially Chris).

CHAPTER 13

Philip White had been born in Essex in 1946, and had gone on to study at the London School of Economics.

From 1969 he had started practising as a surveyor/valuer for a nationwide residential mortgage firm, but since the mid-1980s he had become a director of Southern Properties as well, leaving the said nationwide mortgage firm shortly afterwards.

After Trevor Eagles had died, he had become the sole principal of the firm.

The firm owned property as far north as Yorkshire and as far west as Bristol (the majority being standard family-sized houses to let), but also on the books were some higher-class properties abroad.

Whilst still MRICS-qualified, his days of 'churning out the mortgage valuations' were long gone, and he now divided his time between the management of the above-mentioned portfolio and playing golf.

His eight-hour flight to Fort Myers had been pretty uneventful (apart from a bit of air turbulence towards the end) and as he landed hoped he would be able to get a round or two in whilst in the Sunshine State (he currently played off a handicap of 20, but was hoping to get that down a bit before he reached his fiftieth).

He did not own any property in the USA as such, but the decision had been taken to operate a franchise business over there, and Martin Tyler had been appointed a few years ago to act as his manager.

He usually confined his contact to succinct phone calls, maximum twice a week, but with additional ad hoc trips in between, as he liked to keep things to an orderly routine if he possibly could, but this trip had been dropped on him out of the blue.

On 27 March (pm), he had had a phone call from Goulding and Co.'s Mr R. H. Clarke.

CHAPTER 13A

Within the last 24/36 hours, Robert Hubert Clarke had received several personal phone calls.

Now 60, he had been thinking of retiring from the firm that he had served man and boy for, at Christmas, but now he wondered why he had waited so long (or whether he would ever live to see a long and happy retirement).

His last meeting of the morning seemed to suggest that, despite his and 'the Ring's' best endeavours to cover their tracks, he was (and they were) on the brink of being exposed.

Time, therefore, he thought, to bring out the big guns – no choice; he rang up George Williamson on his private line and got through straight away.

His thoughts were exactly the same – send in Philip White to silence those who were likely to talk; obviously they had not silenced Adam Best early enough, and so if they could close the possible loophole in Florida all might still be well.

This meant that Penny Banks would have to go as well, but they had enough on White from days gone by to ensure that he would sort things out, personally if necessary.

It was therefore early on Tuesday 30 March that Philip White made his twice-weekly call to Martin Tyler (but this time he had a much more sinister reason for calling).

CHAPTER 13B

Having spoken to Martin, Phil White leant back on his brand new real leather office chair and considered the position (both as a whole and in respect of his own career role in the matter).

Things had started off well enough, but then he had, naively to say the least, become involved with Trevor Eagles at Southern Properties, and before he knew it he had been 'well paid' for 'massaging some figures' over a few mortgage valuations.

Nothing had ever been discovered by the authorities (ie the banks or the police), and more work was put his way.

However, it was soon made abundantly clear to him that he had now 'made his bed and must lie on it', otherwise he would be exposed for mortgage fraud (and the threats that followed made it plain that he was now up to his neck in it and couldn't get out of it alive: "So you may as well take the rewards and keep shtum," said Clarke and Williamson together).

Whilst he was not the brainiest person in the world, even he could see that he could now only 'join them not beat them', so he said yes – as a result he had amassed a tidy fortune very quickly, and had soon became a key cog in the Ring's workings.

In 1978, Jon Armstrong had had to be silenced (thank God that that had not been down to him personally, he thought) and the truth had not come out then (due to Steven Johns having become unwittingly involved as a convenient stooge) so why should it now?

Then he had been told to sort out Adam Best (he didn't even know the chap but had arranged that [indirectly] at the end of January, as requested).

And now Penny Banks, but why? – she wasn't the one who was now raking up the past; presumably it was the guy who had been found guilty who was now after justice, (or perhaps it is just a question of her knowing too much after all this time).

Still, his was not to reason why; his was just to do (rather than die).

CHAPTER 14

Vanessa Downing, born 1928, had certainly slept around a bit in her younger days – one of her first partners had been solicitor Robert Clarke.

She had also been friends with George Williamson, but since the late sixties all three had put aside their personal 'likings' and discussed forming the Ring (following a chance get-together whilst on a weekend conference in London).

Coincidentally, all had, within the space of a few weeks, inherited their parents' estates, and at some time during the late evening (probably after several bottles of wine had been quaffed) an idea had arisen of how they could maximise the capital receipt by avoiding paying the inheritance tax due.

Having found this relatively easy to accomplish, they then became cocky and decided to expand their illicit operation by forming the mortgage fraud ring (but it obviously needed other professionals to be involved to make it work).

It was from this first meeting that White had been pressganged into service.

They had deliberately kept 'the Ring' low on numbers – the more that were involved, the more chance there was of a wrong word getting out.

However, Trevor Eagles was brought in (a trader well known to Vanessa) – his company was used to launder the money.

It was generally accepted between the main 'gang of three' that Vanessa Downing was the Ring's leader.

Later on, Martin Tyler's USA franchise business was set up as an additional money laundering outlet.

Since then, all had gone onto bigger and better things (especially Downing and Williamson) but the Ring was still active and it had of course made all its members into multi-millionaires.

After Trevor Eagles died, in 1988, Phil White was placed in sole charge of Southern Properties and, whilst not being a member of the Ring as such, was clearly still associated with all of them, and was well paid for what he continued to do on their behalf.

In the early afternoon of Friday 25 March 1993, Clarke and Williamson updated Vanessa Downing on the latest developments.

CHAPTER 15

After Steve and Martin's quick word on 2 April, the latter set off to pick White up from the airport. They had not gone into a lot of detail, and Steve had been clear to tell Martin that he had to remain non-existent as far as Philip White was concerned.

Martin said he would ensure that there were no slip ups, but wanted to find out why White had come over – concern for Penny presumably as a caring and responsible employer. If only he knew! thought Steve.

Phil White's orders were simple enough – see what is going on out there; we cannot afford Southern Property's franchise business to be blown wide open. Penny Banks might give away some details, so it's time she was dealt with. Please terminate, for the usual fee – money available to hire whoever. Better do a complete job this time (or else your mum might suddenly have a nasty accident one dark night sometime soon).

He had shuddered at this last remark – he had never married and had accordingly remained very close to his mum as she meant the world to him.

"Hello, Martin," said White, smiling (rather forcibly, it seemed to the former). "Are you well – all things considered, of course?" he added hurriedly, almost as an afterthought. "I heard about Penny. Terrible news, wasn't it? How is she? We'll have a quick coffee and then you can fill me in before I call to see her – if she's up to receiving visitors, that is. How's the office?"

Martin smiled back as they shook hands (whilst thinking: loads of questions – why don't I get a chance to answer one before he asks another? He realised at that moment just how much he had always detested him). The sooner he was on the plane back to GB the better – Phil White, of course, had other ideas (like how he was going to 'deal with' Penny Banks as instructed without Martin knowing).

"The office is fine," replied Martin, as the waiter came to the table, deciding to answer his last question first, and get onto the other aspects later (possibly). "Had a punter in only this morning who is interested in some of our property – acting anonymously for person or persons unknown. Still, I guess it doesn't matter as long as he is 'in funds'."

"Fine, well done," said White (but for once his mind was on things other than pounds and pence). "But I would like to go and see Penny straight away before talking shop – just give me her home address and I'll see you back at the office at, say, 1800 hours."

CHAPTER 15A

Chris thought it was time they made for home. "I appreciate that you are still concerned about Penny, to some extent," she said to Steve on the morning of 2 April, "but I don't think that there is anything more she can/will tell you about the Ring etc., and I don't need to know anything else about her relationship with Jon."

Steve was deep in thought, but Chris's words brought him back down to earth with a bump. After quite a long pause he said, "Okay, but I would like to have one more go at her first. Perhaps if I visit her on my own, she may let something slip."

"I very much doubt it," said Chris, "but as you wish – I will see about flights home this afternoon. What about a quick walk along the beach first – I think we both need a breath of air, and a stretch of our legs. In the heat of the day, I know, but I want to top up my tan."

Steve agreed, and they duly left their motel room.

At that very moment, Martin was pulling up outside Penny's house, and entered by the back door. He had a sixth sense that Philip White was up to no good; he didn't know what he could do, but was determined to get into the house first, just in case.

Penny was asleep, then came a knock at the door, followed by another, harder one. That must be him now, thought Martin; he's obviously impatient. He moved to the door, his muscles tensed and ready to go…

He opened the door, but it was only the nurse for Penny's daily physiotherapy.

Whilst she was administering the same in the bedroom, Steve rang the doorbell. Martin was as surprised to see Steve as he was him.

Obviously Steve couldn't really ask Penny owt of any significance now, so he made an excuse that he was just calling to say cheerio (as Chris was now keen to get home etc.), but then asked if he had broached the subject of property with Philip White.

"Not yet," said Martin. "He wanted to see Penny first – said he would meet me back at the office after 6pm. So far, however, he hasn't shown up here – in fact, I thought it was he ringing the doorbell just then, and not you."

Both somewhat perplexed, they sat until the nurse had finished and then all three left together to go their separate ways.

"I'll let you know tomorrow if there is any property news from the office after 6pm – I will be working till late tonight anyway by the looks of it, I would think," Martin grinned.

They set off together, but Steve pulled up round the corner, parked and peered round a group of palm trees (he thought of returning to Chris there and then, but felt he had to try and speak to Penny again whilst at the same time being ultra-cautious if Philip White was on his way).

Bullseye! His sixth sense was right: that must be him arriving now, late on purpose to try and catch us out. Well, not me, matey – time for a chat, methinks, he thought as he moved back to the rear of Penny's house.

Phil White was quite calm on the outside, but inside he was shaking like a leaf.

His instructions related to Penny only, but he had decided on his drive out to see her just to visit and adopt a caring employer role (whilst pumping her for info) then report back to the Ring/employ a hitman to do the rest.

That way he might be able to first glean if anyone else knew too much – ie Martin (thus getting a feather in his cap in the eyes of his lords and masters) – that way they might leave his adopted mum alone, at least for the foreseeable future.

He went to the front door, and finding it unlocked went inside – only for him to receive what felt like a hammer blow to the side of his head, and he passed out.

CHAPTER 16

"Mr Clarke, I presume."

Reg had decided to take the bull by the horns and call into Goulding and Co.'s offices on the Friday dinnertime (following Steve's call at the crack of dawn regarding the attack on Penny Banks etc.) as he had had no joy in getting Clarke on the phone.

Based on his words he had just had with Steve, he felt he had to do something more at the GB end than hitherto.

His research into the Ring had not proved very informative, but, based on how they were getting on in Florida, the Ring's inclusion of Vanessa Downing, his feelings for Chris; all these aspects leant heavily on his shoulders (but the one thing he was determined to do above all else was support his nephew 110 per cent in clearing his name).

He would like to get them back from Florida so he could look after them (and see more of Chris into the bargain!) as he thought the Penny Banks aspect was small fry.

He was 100 per cent sure that the Ring was at the heart of this mess, and furthermore would have bet his last buck that it was all Downing's doing – he had met her once, a long time ago when he was in his early thirties, briefly –

ie a one-night stand – at some high-society ex-army do in London, and didn't like what he saw (but at that age all that mattered to him was the sex so he didn't really care about her other attributes, or rather the lack of them).

He didn't know much about George Williamson's past life but adding two and two together guessed Vanessa Downing had got some sort of hold on him (and Robert Clarke as well in all probability).

Would confronting Clarke head on therefore 'blow the investigation' and furthermore put Steve and Chris in mortal danger?

He realised that was the $64,000 dollar question firmly in front of him – maybe it was his love for Chris that caused him to dither over what to do next but his investigations had come to a stop regarding Philip White and his love for his nephew had to take priority – *"blood runs thicker than water"* and all that.

Robert Clarke peered up and over his spectacles and looked Reg up and down. He had had a long career and was racking his brains to try and recall if he should remember him from the dim and distant past.

His secretary had not been very enlightening in making the appointment, and he didn't usually agree to diary dates being fixed for Fridays as he liked to get away early to his holiday home in the country by mid-afternoon, but he had been more than a little intrigued with the surname – could it possibly be anything to do with the Steven Johns 'frame-up' of 1978/9? he wondered. He had to check it out just in case, as steps would have to be put in place if that proved to be the case, especially following the news coming back from Florida about the apparently botched Banks elimination; therefore he had agreed to see him.

"How can I help you, Mr Johns? I'm about to have an early lunch so I trust that you can be brief."

Reg sat down and nodded a yes to the proffered coffee. "Hopefully what I have come to ask you shouldn't take long, Mr Clarke (time being money and all that). I'm here on a private matter following a recommendation by a distant relative in the matter of planning law. I have several investments, including a site in the East Midlands which I can't seem to get planning permission for. The local county council seem reluctant to agree to my proposals, and I want to know what my chances are if I were to appeal to the secretary of state for the environment."

Reg had been thinking on his feet a bit as he started talking – granted, he had had plenty of time to consider his words carefully but had decided at the last minute that he must make some bold move at his end to help Steve's case.

He watched for any reaction whilst he was talking, but there was nothing noticeable from the other side of the desk so he continued.

"I don't know the secretary of state personally, of course – the Right Honourable George Williamson MP, if I remember rightly, but wondered if your firm are able to take this case on for me? At the right fee, of course!" He flashed a smile as he finished.

"I'm sorry, Mr Johns, but I don't specialise in planning appeals – my forte is personal injury claims, etc., and I prefer to stick to what I know at my time of life."

He smiled (but inwardly he was thinking, it's got to be the same Johns – maybe not the same person as such as this guy is far too old to be the 22-year-old youth who we got sent down but got to be the same family – reference to a county council and the Department of the Environment by name can't be just coincidence. I reckon they are onto us after all; God knows how. Got to ring the others as soon as I can get rid of him).

"Furthermore," he continued, "the main partner here at Gouldings who would have been able to help you has just retired, so I fear you have had a wasted journey." He paused, then added, "I don't get involved with the politics of life, but is there anything else I can help you with at all?" as he belatedly offered his business card.

Reg had just finished his coffee, so stood up to leave. "No, I don't either – never trust a politician, I always say, whether they are Tory or otherwise. Sorry to have wasted your valuable time, Mr Clarke, but do want to get planning permission for my site as I don't think the leader of the county council has been acting appropriately. I'm sure I'll find another lawyer – thanks for your card; may be useful if I ever have a personal injury claim!" he joked as he offered a farewell handshake.

Robert Clarke returned the traditional goodbye gesture, and showed him to the door. "Goodbye, Mr Johns, sorry I couldn't be of more assistance."

"Have a nice weekend away in the country, Mr Clarke," replied Steve.

CHAPTER 16A

Reg could hardly contain his satisfaction – back in the car he switched on his receiver and tuned into the bugging device he had managed to plant in Clarke's office.

True, it had been a risky strategy, mentioning names etc. but felt he was involved up to his neck, and hoped he would soon have some proof to take to the cops.

He lit his pipe up and waited.

After about half an hour of immaterial phone calls and dictation, he jerked in his seat as he heard Clarke speaking about his visit. Couldn't be sure who he was speaking to at first, but his final "Goodbye, George" clinched it.

Got him – but then his joy immediately turned to horror as, just as he was about to turn his receiver off, he picked up Clarke's call to Philip White, instructing him to "Go to Florida and sort out all outstanding matters, otherwise your mum might meet with a very nasty accident."

"What have I done?" Reg thought. "No doubt they will be sending someone for me as well now – remains to be seen, but all I can do now is to go over to Florida myself and try to prevent more loss of life before it's too late."

He drove round the corner, found the nearest travel agent and booked himself on the first available flight to Miami – 2 April (not knowing that sat on the very same plane would be one Philip White, MRICS).

CHAPTER 17

Philip White stirred, and didn't like what he saw – how many of the buggers are there?

He thought he had worked it so he would just be able to question Penny Banks on her own, then see Martin Tyler back at his office, hire a hitman as necessary and then hightail it back to dear old Blighty, report in and then get to his mum's.

Obviously he had been sussed out, and followed. He swore he'd get Tyler for this – but first how would he talk his way out of this situation (without him having to tell all) alive?

He concluded that his chances of doing that looked very slim indeed from where he lay.

"Allow me to do the introductions," said a voice from the shadows. Steve stepped forward, and in that instant White knew he was doomed.

"I am Steven Johns. Remember that name, Mr White?" It got worse. "And this is Mrs Christine Armstrong – remember Mr Jon Armstrong, Mr White? Penny Banks you already know, presumably…"

The door burst open and Reg entered. "And I am Mr Reginald Johns' senior," he announced, slightly out of breath. "We haven't met before, of course."

Steve was absolutely stunned; Chris fainted.

"And you all know who I am," said the last entrant (Martin had just got back to Penny's to see Reg enter, and rushed over to try and surprise him from behind, but failed). "What the hell is going on in my fiancée's house?"

"Now that's a very good question," said Steve. "Most of us know why we're here Martin, that is apart from you yourself of course! Allow me to apologise for not being straight with you earlier, but I had no choice, as you will see when I tell you the whole story. But first, Uncle Reg, how the hell did you know to come here?"

It took about one hour for first Steve, then Christine and finally Reg to go through the history lesson with a fine-toothed comb, ending with the account of the detailed happenings of the past week, days and hours.

Martin was not impressed with the facts as presented regarding his fiancée and he was also none too happy with Steve's earlier deceptions towards him but seemed to accept that Philip White had been up to no good from the start.

Notwithstanding, he had listened intently to said recap, as had Penny.

The latter was still coming to terms with the recent attack on her, and the resulting (likely permanent) disability, and although she realised (now if not before) why she had been attacked and was now very worried about how Martin would react to him having been told of her past life. What with her disability, would he want her anymore?

She noted he still referred to her as his fiancée, which was perhaps encouraging, but she couldn't imagine (when all the dust had settled) that he really meant it (and who could blame him – he had been done up like a kipper by Philip White [and her to some extent] with the property shop franchise business, not to mention Steve's aforementioned apology).

"Right then," said Steve, taking charge (at least 'the Plan' that he had been thinking about for so long whilst in Inverness Jail was starting to yield some progress – but what would the results be?). "Mr White and Ms Banks to start, I think."

CHAPTER 18

Vanessa Downing was now leader of Herts County Council, aged 65 years old. She regarded it as the pinnacle of her long (and distinguished) career.

She had been a member of the Tory Party for as long as she could remember (certainly from the early 1950s) – Harold Macmillan had been her hero (her parents had been very good friends with him). She came from a particularly wealthy background but her parents had lost almost everything in the never had it so good post-war years (from which they never really recovered) and this made her more determined than ever to succeed in life, whatever it took, to make up for that.

Sadly, that had not fully happened before both her parents had died suddenly in 1966, during the years of Harold Wilson's Labour government (although there was by then something of an estate to deal with).

She was the sole executor and beneficiary thereof.

She had got to know Robert Clarke and George Williamson socially in the 1950s but it was not until after her parents died that she started her plan to make her fortune.

First there was the inheritance tax loophole, followed by savings on capital gains tax – it just seemed to snowball from there really into 'the Ring'. Nowadays, legal restrictions make mortgage fraud much more difficult to get through without being caught but back then, when estate agents could also organise the mortgage valuation on the property they had just sold, much could be done by the criminally minded to abuse the system (if they were so inclined).

Certainly Trevor Eagles, and latterly Philip White, had been key players, resulting in massive funds having been accumulated for all of them.

Then, on 27 March, she had been contacted by Robert and George.

She had always prided herself that she had always been on top of the situation, whilst at the same time being sufficiently remote from the goings on the ground should things go pear-shaped at any time.

Obviously she now realised that that assumption may have proved to be somewhat erroneous. She had thought that getting rid of Adam Best had nipped it all in the bud, but it seemed that he had given information away (how he had got it God knows) before that.

Obviously this Steven Johns was now out to clear his name for the Jon Armstrong murder, but what info had he got? It seems that he knew about Robert and George, but her?

I need to refine my exit strategy, just in case all the shit hits the fan, she thought. The other two can carry the can for this. I'm going to wangle my way out of this one somehow, but it's too late to think of taking Penny with me – she will just have to "go down with the others now in order that I can save my own skin.

She rang them both back with their instructions – Johns must be silenced at all costs.

After putting the phone down, Robert Clarke thought to himself, That's all very well, but what about Johns' senior? He's as dangerous as anyone, but we can't eliminate everyone. Then pure panic took over, and he rushed to the loo before he shat himself.

CHAPTER 18A

George Williamson was the real villain of the piece – outwardly cool, calm and collected, not to mention being academically gifted in the extreme, he was as hard as nails underneath his immaculate three-piece and dicky bow, and would have sold his own grandma down the river for ten bob if he thought he could get away with it. Okay, he thought, it had been Vanessa's idea initially, but I was the one that made it all come together and tick so as to get the money rolling in – if it hadn't been for me the actual theory would never have been turned into hard cash."

His outwardly honest political role as secretary of state had eventually been procured following years of contacts, calling in favours and bribes to get what he wanted: power.

Yes, his millions had bought him that to some extent but in order to wield real political power the greasing of palms was needed.

He had no compunction at all in doing this and in his eyes the end goal justified any means, end of – the old maxim that power corrupts and absolute power corrupts absolutely could be no better illustrated.

CHAPTER 19

Reg's family history searches had begun shortly after his brother had died in 1966. It had taken him to various archive centres across various parts of southern Britain, but mainly in the county of Essex.

Although he had gone back over 200 years, he had found nothing out of the ordinary, eg adulterous affairs, bigamy, children born out of wedlock etc., in his immediate family, and, having come to something of a full stop over further progress, he had left the whole thing in limbo (to come back to in his retirement perhaps) following his recent success in being awarded new employment contracts abroad.

His recent research tracing members of 'the Ring' had, in a funny sort of way, galvanised his interest in pursuing his own ancestry further in early course (but this would have to wait until all the current problems had been unravelled).

As he stood in the shadows of Penny Banks's front room in sunny Florida, he couldn't help but think of Chris, as opposed to Steve, a thought which didn't exactly fill him with too much family pride.

He had had a big stroke of luck at Gatwick in that he had overheard the check-in staff referring to Philip White by name, and he had therefore stuck to him like glue thereafter. He had lost him when he was being met by Martin Tyler, but then caught up with his movements later and duly followed him out to Penny Banks's house.

He had also formed an immediate dislike to White – one of those slimy 'Uriah Heep'-type characters, and was not at all surprised of his involvement in the Ring.

Where, he wondered, was all this going to lead, and how would it all unfold? Not easy to resolve here in Florida under US laws, that's for sure.

Martin was all for calling for the cops – he had listened intently to the history lesson and couldn't believe everything he was hearing (it's the sort of thing you watch late at night at the cinema, he thought).

But then he thought his complicity with Philip White over his property franchise might be of more than a passing interest to the local sheriff than some of the other stuff he had just been listening to, and as he was the only American present he decided to hold back on that one.

He couldn't believe all that had been said about Penny, though – how could she not have confided in him? And look at her now – paralysed for life.

"So," said Steve, bringing everyone back to reality with a jolt, "talk yourself out of this one if you can "Perry", what have you got to say for yourself, Mr White?"

CHAPTER 19A

The evening had long since passed into the small hours of 3 April. It had certainly been a long day for everyone, but especially for yesterday's two airborne travellers.

As they all stared down at Philip White, Penny stirred in her wheelchair and their gaze shifted onto her. Phil White's natural instinct was to deny all knowledge of the Ring, and just admit to employing Martin Tyler to run the American arm of Southern Properties. However, Penny Banks spoke first – mainly directed at Martin (not surprisingly).

"I came originally from England, Martin, as you know. I trained as an independent financial advisor upon leaving school. In the mid-seventies I was still 'learning the ropes' but my mum kept pushing me to work harder and harder, and that included working for Southern Properties as well for a spell."

She paused and looked at Christine specifically for a split second, then continued, "Through my work I met Jon and…" She started sobbing. "Yes, we started seeing each other, but then when he died –" full-scale blubbing now "– I panicked and got out of GB as quickly as I could.

"I'm so sorry, Christine, so very, very sorry, but I didn't have anything to do with Jon's death (let alone the subsequent trial etc.). That's clear if only because of the attack on me just over one week ago – if I was a main member of 'the Ring', or whatever you call it, then why was I targeted for elimination?"

She started a coughing fit, and Martin moved closer to her. "I am very grateful of course to you two for turning up when you did to apprehend the hitman but I don't know anything else except Philip White here was an employee of Southern Properties, working for Mr Trevor Eagles originally, and they gradually provided us here in Naples with a good number of properties to let, which was all good business for us so we just rolled our sleeves up and got cracking. The commission rate was good and we both enjoyed our work, only for it to come to this…"

She looked down at her lifeless legs, then concluded, "Other than that, I don't know what else to say, Martin, except I still love you and please don't leave me."

There was a long pause, then the start of slow, sarcastic applause from Steve, but before he or Martin could react further Reg jumped into the fray.

"Steve, I know what you are going to say, but first I think we should press Philip White for some answers." Steve hesitated, but then nodded his agreement to Reg, proceeding as he had just suggested so Reg edged round in his chair to face Philip White.

"Mr White, I warn you now that we already know quite a bit about you so I would suggest you think very carefully about the answers you are about to give."

He paused to allow his opening statement to sink in, then said, "I am not suggesting you killed Jon Armstrong, but am suggesting you were instructed/hired to get rid of

Penny Banks here to stop the Ring's identity from getting out, but that was botched, wasn't it, and, thanks to Steve and Christine here, she survived. True or false?"

CHAPTER 19B

Phil White rose from his seat – he always felt that looking up at others whilst talking always put one at an immediate disadvantage – much better to be on a level playing field (height-wise, at the very least) when trying to put over a convincing argument.

"In a word, true – BUT before you all pile on me and throw me to the lions perhaps I can explain my predicament in all of this." As there was no immediate counter to this, or follow-up questions, he continued with his pre-planned version of events.

"I was originally a regular chartered surveyor carrying out residential surveys and mortgage valuations in Essex and the Home Counties. My work brought me into contact with a lot of people, and before I knew it I was 'helping oil the wheels of progress' by ensuring that money continued to 'make the world go round'. The trouble was that my mother became ill, and she had no one else to pay for her care, so I 'joined up' with Southern Properties to try and earn some extra fee income – the downside to that though was, Mr Trevor Eagles soon had me by the short and curlies for carrying out some favourable mortgage valuations for him, and as he threatened me with my mum's future non-well-being I was caught up in his ever-increasing web of deceit.

I met Jon Armstrong occasionally –" he glanced at Christine momentarily "– but I am not aware that he was involved like I was.

However, despite Penny Banks's denials a few moments ago, I can confirm that she does know more than she is letting on because she was involved with Southern Properties in setting up his office here in Florida." He looked at Martin. "Yes, your office, Martin."

Both Penny and Martin tried to interrupt him at this point but White wouldn't give way, and continued, "You can deny it all you want, duck, but it's a fact – you were involved in the mortgage fraud ring (because that's what it was, and is), whereas I have been manipulated by others, eg Trevor Eagles, into a situation where I had no choice but to comply with my instructions otherwise my mum would have been got rid of."

It was Steve who then took control – 'the List' given to him that cold and wet January night in Leith by Adam Best seemed a lifetime ago now but loomed large in his thoughts as he said, "Both you and Penny were on a list I compiled some time ago and as far as I am concerned (from what you have said both today and previously) you are both implicated in the Ring (and therefore Jon Armstrong's death, albeit indirectly). I accept some of what you both say, but not the majority, but also accept that neither of you were the ringleaders. However, what I demand to know, before I turn you both over to the authorities, is who the said ringleaders are."

"I only knew of Trevor Eagles," said White straight away, "and that's the God's honest truth, so help me God."

Penny was silent, but it was obvious from his looks that Martin was starting to believe Penny's involvement in all of this was not just around the edges.

"I don't believe you," replied Steve. "I suggest, Philip, that when this thing goes public your beloved mother will be in more danger then than she is now. As far as you are concerned, Penny, I would suggest that, if you are sincere in your feelings for Martin here, you will also cooperate fully, as you are in more danger of losing his affections if you don't than if you do."

"I don't believe you either," said Reg. "Does the name Robert Hubert Clarke ring any bells at all?"

White winced but then replied, "Don't you see? I have already said too much – my safety and more importantly that of my mum is already in serious danger from what I have just said."

"But, as I said at the beginning, Mr White, you are in equal danger now if you don't cooperate with us. I repeat, do you know Mr Robert Hubert Clarke, solicitor, of Goulding and Co.?"

He slowly sank back into his chair – he knew the game was up. He looked at Reg, Steve and Christine in turn, sighed and then nodded a yes.

"At last," yelped Steve, but Reg then continued, "You have at least started to cooperate, but I know about Robert Clarke's involvement already. However, you may find the next lot of information more interesting." He then proceeded to play back the bugged telephone calls involving Clarke, Williamson and White himself. When he had finished, Reg said (mainly to White but also to Penny), "So you see, Mr White, *we* now have *you* by the short and curlies so please be cooperative by telling us all you know about George Williamson."

Both of them denied knowing anything about him (and for once Reg and Steve tended to believe them). Then Steve said, "There is another name on my list which hasn't been mentioned yet – a Mrs Vanessa Downing."

At that point Penny screamed out, "That's my mum."

CHAPTER 19C

There was a mass chorus of OMGs from Steve and Chris together, but Reg had gone a deathly white: surely it's impossible; how could fate have dealt him such a hand as this? In 1952 he had been 31 and she would have been about 24 or so – the dates therefore seemed to match to circa nine months before her birth.

Reg couldn't believe it (and he couldn't see much family likeness either) but he thought that Penny was probably telling the truth (and, what's more, he was her dad!).

But, having looked across at Steve and then Penny, he chose to say nothing.

Steve was beaming from ear to ear; talk about a family business – Adam Best couldn't have known all this (could he?) but he had certainly come up with the goods, list-wise. In his eyes, everyone thereon had now been accounted for; it was just a case of seeing justice done and then he could get on with the rest of his life – he looked across at Chris and wondered if she really would be willing to spend it with him here in south-west Florida.

Chris and Martin stood rooted to the spot as though momentarily frozen in time. Chris thought Penny would now be finally punished for what she had done to her beloved Jon all those years ago (although, now the time had finally arrived, victory didn't seem to be as sweet as she had imagined it would be). Martin thought that nothing was sweet anymore, particularly anything British – he had been fine working in what for him had been a high-powered job in property – up until a few weeks ago, that is. Now it had all been wrecked by more than one British crook. He glanced at Penny, who was still screaming on about her mum, and thought that their partnership couldn't go on.

It was however Philip White who was first to actually respond. "I told you all I was not directly responsible for all of this – it's such as her over there and Vanessa Downing you need to blame."

"Oh no you don't," snarled Steve. "Don't think you can wriggle out of any involvement just because of what Penny has just said. You'll get what's coming to you, don't worry about that, irrespective of her role in all of this – it changes nothing as far as you are concerned."

Reg still said nothing... all he could think about was the recalling of his afterthought following his chat with Steve on 21 February: "Vanessa Downing, eh, now there's a blast from the past – I could soon be between a 'rock and a hard place' in all of this but, what the hell, family comes first and anyway I owe it to his dad to help Steve whatever the personal sacrifice to me."

How prophetic these random thoughts were proving to be now (but family coming first had just taken on a whole new meaning – daughter or nephew certainly compared to rocks and hard places).

CHAPTER 19D

"So, Penny, what's your full family details?" demanded Steve.

"I married Vinny Banks in 1976, but my maiden name was Downing – I never knew my father…"

At that point Reg started spluttering and coughing, but pointed to his pipe that he had just got on the go as being the reason for his sudden coughing fit (as opposed to Penny's last statement being the true cause).

"My marriage didn't last long—"

"I'm not surprised," burst out Christine.

"—but then managed to get a job in property at Southern Properties Limited with Trevor Eagles. From what has been said here over the last few hours I realise now that it was only because of my mother having a hold on Eagles that I got the job (and others since, probably, including this one here in the States, Martin) but I repeat I did *not* kill Jon Armstrong or knowingly assist in anyway. I did like Jon though, Christine, and admit I did give him the come-on, but one thing's now certain to me above everything else, which is that anything I can do to ensure my mum and all her other helpers 'go to hell' forever I will gladly now do without hesitation."

"Okay," said Reg, having recovered a bit from the shock news. "I think it is crystal clear that we have done all we can here Steve – it's obvious that Penny is telling the truth now: your plan/list has been confirmed, and what's more we have more evidence than we'd ever thought we'd get on the ringleaders so let's quit whilst we are ahead, get back to dear old Blighty and leave the authorities to deal with all the formalities (before the ringleaders set up further ambushes for us all)."

Steve glanced at his watch and noted that it was now 4am local time on 3 April 1993 (well past his and, he suspected, everybody else's normal bedtime) but didn't immediately respond as he was suddenly aware of a slight (barely perceptible) change in his uncle's demeanour – he couldn't quite put his finger on it at that precise moment, and could have been imagining it at that time of the morning after such a long and frenetic day, but... "Anything wrong, Unc?"

"Wrong? How can anything be wrong with me given what we have heard tonight?" He paused momentarily, then said, "I just think that, of all those on the list, Penny is the least to blame and given what has happened to her courtesy of Philip White's hitman, she deserves our help in some small way – I know, Chris, you probably won't agree with that because that's the main reason you came over to Florida but surely, Steve, you can see what I mean... can't you?"

Steve didn't reply, but it had now just been confirmed to him that Reg's preferences had moved too much in Penny's favour (and at his expense).

CHAPTER

England, dear old England – even though at 30,000 feet he could see nothing of it yet for all the rainclouds (good old April showers). It was now early morning (BST) on 6 April – flights back from Florida were usually overnighters, and touchdown was apparently about 30 minutes away.

All of this was not particularly unusual when any plane travels anticlockwise to the UK, but following all that had happened in the States since 20 March, what was unusual was that of the original four fairly recent outward-bound flight passengers only two were returning (Reg and Chris).

The facts of the matter were that on 5 April Steve and Reg had had a blazing row. Chris had kept out of it – she had already said she was ready to go home, and the happenings of 2 and 3 April had not radically changed such a view (re Penny and Jon anyway).

Although she had enjoyed Florida very much, it could not compensate her for her reason for having gone there in the first place. Somewhat sadistically, I suppose, she had seen Penny Banks get her 'just desserts' – whilst not wishing paralysis on anybody, perhaps it was God's way of having his revenge (for Jon's sake?).

Reg and Steve seemed to suddenly be at odds over how to take the whole matter forward. It was obvious that Reg seemed to be showing a massive concern for Penny all of a sudden, but why? Was it just because she was now paralysed, and had inadvertently been in the wrong place at the wrong time, or was there something more to it than that?

This is what Steve seemed to be taking exception to, anyway – he was still set in his single-minded approach to seeing all those responsible for his false imprisonment etc. receiving the full force of the law (understandable, yes, but surely not to the extent of turning on his uncle like he did).

I suppose something had to give, but Chris had never seen two family members go at it like they had – it was a wonder they both didn't have cardiac arrests on the spot.

From Reg's perspective, the reasons were obvious (to him) but he couldn't let on as to why just yet to Steve – too ashamed, he guessed, but anyway, daughter or no daughter, she and her birth mother were now proved to be two of the main culprits in Steve's frame-up.

Such a predicament – he wanted to back Steve, of course, but 'family ties' had for him taken on a whole new meaning.

Steve had had this sixth sense for a while now, and Reg's reaction when he alluded to such doubts about Penny's knowing involvement in all of this now proved, to him at least, that something was badly wrong. Most weird, but now he had got so far with his plan and 'the List' he couldn't allow any family arguments to get in his way (whatever his respect for Reg was).

Eventually, via 'an uneasy truce', it had been agreed that Steve would stay in America (to tie up loose ends regarding

Philip White, 'build bridges' with Martin and arrange some further paliative care for Penny), whereas Reg would accompany Chris home, get her to a safe house if necessary and then be available to further the investigation of Robert Clarke, George Williamson and Vanessa Downing (via the police, the Fraud Squad, Interpol, whoever).

That did give Reg the added bonus of being with Chris for a bit longer, of course, but obviously the downside was he had had to leave his "daughter of recent acquaintance" behind. "Supposed to be an expert genealogist and yet I couldn't even discover that I had had a daughter of my own, albeit an illegitimate one. Bloody useless or what?"

CHAPTER 20A

So now there were only three left on the list that were still at large, but the net was closing in.

On the basis that Penny for certain and Phil White quite possibly would both testify against them, and with Martin's back-up evidence, Steve was quietly confident that they had gathered enough (circumstantial at least) evidence to at least convince the CPS that there was a case to answer in any average English courtroom (and hopefully achieve a guilty verdict as a result).

However, evidence was the keyword – he reflected on the fact that the authorities hadn't had that much when he was convicted in 1979.

Perhaps 1993 was different – but just what had they actually got on the three ringleaders? Some bugged evidence, and Philip White's testimony against Robert Clarke but for the other two (apart from Penny being ready to testify against her own mother) precious little when one comes to analyse things in a lot more detail.

The fact that they were on some list provided by previous jailbird Adam Best was a bit tenuous to say the least.

In fact, when you come to think about it, 'the List' was not even in Adam Best's handwriting but Steve's!

Whilst we have them on the ropes, we are far from achieving a KO blow, probably not even in the last round yet, he mused as he pushed Penny round the block in her wheelchair for a quick breath of afternoon air.

On his return, the nurse was waiting to arrange some more treatment at the hospital for her.

CHAPTER 21

Reg and Chris got through customs quite quickly, and they both headed back to hers (automatic pilot – nothing said, just an instinctive thing).

Once there, Chris let Steve know they had got back okay and after a late brunch they started to get down to some detailed discussions on making further progress with the authorities (whilst thinking about their own protection from the Ring's members at the same time).

Their eyes suddenly met, and Chris said, "What has happened between the two of you? This thing has started to poison all of us."

Reg couldn't help it – for the first time in his 70-odd years he completely broke down and sobbed uncontrollably. Eventually, he was able to pull himself together a bit to utter a few disjointed words and phrases, which included his feelings for her but perhaps, more importantly, the news he had recently learnt about Penny and Vanessa Downing and his resulting dilemma about his daughter and nephew.

Chris was dumbstruck, more about the latter than the former, and didn't know what to say for the best. She tried to comfort him with some appropriate platitudes but Reg just sat there, slumped in his chair and feeling every one of his 72 years (and then some). Why do I find both love and that I have a daughter when I am too old to fully enjoy either?" he thought. No justice.

"We can talk about both matters shortly, but first and foremost we are jet lagged in the extreme and desperately need a power nap before we do anything else; you use the spare bedroom and am sure we will both feel a lot better, and think a lot clearer, after that."

However once in her room she rang Steve to try and mend some fences on his behalf but without too much luck initially. He did however eventually agree to come back to the UK, though only after Martin's court appearance next week. "But more to see you again than him."

She didn't tell him about Reg's feelings for her, or Penny being his daughter and Downing being her mother! Not her place and, anyway, both matters not the sort of thing to just come out with over the phone.

When they woke, Reg was feeling quite a bit better – Chris on the other hand (having spoken to Steve and then not being able to drop off thereafter) felt worse.

They started chatting about their feelings for one another and about Penny being Reg's daughter – she decided to tell him she had no feelings for either of them but Penny was more of a problem in her eyes (now not only involved in the Ring and with her deceased husband but a relation to the man she was sitting next to).

She didn't know if she would cope with that but just as she was about to respond further the intercom buzzed and she found that it was the police wanting to come in and take them both down to local cop shop, 'to assist them in their ongoing enquiries'.

So further talk on what to do about the Ring's three top-level members would just have to wait (even if one of those was the mother of Reg's daughter).

CHAPTER 22

Clarke, Williamson and Downing were after all these years in the same room together – one of George's private rooms near the Houses of Parliament.

Not out of his or Vanessa's choice but Robert Clarke had felt he had to push the issue to the brink in order to be get everyone to be able to see the wood from the trees (he had never trusted either of them and felt they were plotting to frame him for the whole thing).

It was Downing who kicked things off. "So, how come they are on to us? Who has talked, and about whom? It is now certain Robert that your name is definitely in the frame – why the hell did you agree to meet this Reg Johns anyway; wasn't it obvious who he was and why he came to see you?"

"I did my best to nip the whole thing in the bud earlier this year," retorted Clarke, "on your orders: you left it to me to deal with Adam Best, and subsequently for Philip White to arrange to silence Penny, if you remember. I sorted the former out well enough, and arranged for the same fate to befall Penny as well for that matter, although as we now know White didn't do what he was supposed to do. So that loophole does still remain, potentially, a big issue, I admit,

IF he talks, but I still think that that is unlikely given the 'family hold' we still have over him."

George chipped in with his two-penneth, "The facts seem to be that someone gave these two Johnses some leads and presumably that was Adam Best sometime between his leaving Inverness Jail and his 'unfortunate disappearance' shortly afterwards. But what we don't know for certain is what the full list of names comprised. We know that you, Robert, were on that list (the bugging device planted in your office was proof of that) but also most probably Philip White and also your daughter, Vanessa."

"As I have said before, George," she replied, "I'm not interested in Penny; all I am bothered about is us."

She meant herself only, of course.

"I think that we have three choices: one, give ourselves up; two, all implement our exit strategies (both of these would immediately be an admission of our guilt); or, three, find a safe bolthole for Robert on the basis that our two names are not in the frame. None is perfect, but if three works Philip White downwards will carry the can. One thing is certain, though: Penny is the major link back to me so she will have to go come what may."

Williamson glanced sideways at Robert Clarke, thinking, she is only after saving herself and getting rid of her daughter in the process. Deluded or what? Robert thought she was in cloud cuckoo land.

CHAPTER 23

Steve was busily trying to wrap things up in Florida quickly (but realised he wasn't able to set the pace of the American legal processes).

Philip White had been duly arrested, awaiting extradition to the UK (hopefully his mother was now under police protection back home). It remained to be seen if he would now talk to the authorities.

Penny had been arrested as well, but released on bail (the court were obviously happy she wasn't going to abscond anywhere!).

So that just left the Martin situation to be dealt with – he just wanted to speak up for him but the local police (in their usual over-the-top 'sledge hammer to crack a nut' way) had arrested him as well. Being the only US citizen in all of this, they were entitled to pursue their own methods, he supposed, but he was pleased that his appeal for bail was due that afternoon, and he was hopeful that he could provide enough of a character witness that would persuade the Florida court to drop all charges.

As he entered the courtroom, however, his mind wandered back to how Chris was doing without him. He then realised just how little Uncle Reg had entered his mind of late.

CHAPTER 23A

It was 6am on 1 May when Steve landed at Gatwick, and as he walked across the tarmac to the arrivals hall noted it looked like it was going to be as nice a day as the one he had left behind in Miami the previous afternoon (early-season heatwave, by the looks of it).

Things had certainly started to happen in the British press big time – details of the Jon Armstrong murder had been re-covered ad nauseum, but now it was linked to the mortgage fraud recently uncovered by the authorities in GB and USA.

Individual names had not been publicly released, of course, neither was there any particular mention of the Adam Best disappearance or the attempted murder of Penny, but he guessed a press embargo had been put in place across the board so as to prevent any rogue journalist or publication from breaking ranks.

However, it made no secret of the fact that the matter was being investigated jointly by the CID and the CIA so it was at least clear that the 'wanted persons list' spanned at least two continents.

Perhaps therefore it was no big surprise that Steve was met by the police on his arrival.

CHAPTER 23B

Although it had been a long day for all of them at their respective police stations (jet lag or no jet lag), by tea time they had all been allowed to leave. As Steve got out onto the street he discovered he had a mini welcoming party in the form of Chris and Reg (who had both been released earlier on in the afternoon and had quickly found out which police station Steve had been taken to).

So, after greeting Chris with hugs and kisses (but just a formal handshake for Reg), he led them across the road to the nearest bar for some of the local amber nectar. Chris followed; Reg momentarily hesitated but then followed Christine's lead.

This is where things are really going to kick off, but perhaps better to get a bit of Dutch courage down my neck first before I tell him he has a cousin and I have a daughter! he thought.

EPILOGUE

Extract from Serious Fraud Office (SFO) press release,
14 December 1993

Eight persons (including the former leader of Hertfordshire County Council Mrs Vanessa Downing and former secretary of state for the environment Mr George Williamson MP) were sentenced yesterday at High Wycombe Crown Court to a total of 45 years' imprisonment for fraud relating to residential mortgage applications by Judge Nicola J Hudson, QC.

The sentences followed a six-week-long trial of three of the defendants, which concluded with guilty verdicts on 4 December 1993 – another five defendants had already admitted their parts in the fraud ahead of the trial. Sentencing took place on 13 December 1993.

Charges against another two persons were dropped before the trial commenced due to lack of evidence.

This is a case about the systemic abuse of the mortgage lending procedure in England and Wales, specifically in relation to a long list of properties as set out in Appendix A attached hereto principally in Yorkshire, Essex and the Home Counties over nearly two and a half decades, and the subsequent laundering of the profits in both Great Britain and the USA.

The essence of the frauds, which were committed on a wholesale basis between 1970 and 1992, was that applications for mortgage advances were made for properties where the sale price quoted in the application was more than the actual price realised on the open market. Fake documents, forged documents and other misleading information supported the applications.

Money acquired through these fraudulent applications was then laundered through the client account of a solicitors' firm to form a massive property portfolio of the principal defendants, both at home and abroad.

The prosecution's case centred on the ringleaders of the whole operation, namely the three defendants who had pleaded not guilty.

The eight defendants in the case were as follows:

- Mr George Williamson, MP and former secretary of state for the environment.
- Mrs Vanessa Downing, the former Conservative leader of Hertfordshire County Council.
- Mr Robert Hubert Clarke, solicitor, of Goulding and Co. of Essex.
- Mr Philip White, chartered surveyor, who carried out the false property valuations and who was the sole proprietor of Southern Properties Ltd, a company set up to organise the money laundering side of the operation, both in the UK and USA.
- Ms Penelope Banks, latterly the main administrator of 'the Ring's' money laundering operation in mid-Florida, USA.

- Mr John Stoddard, a mortgage broker employed by 'the Ring', who put together the mortgage applications.
- Mr Thomas Brown, a conveyancing clerk at Goulding and Co., who played a major role in processing the mortgage applications at Clarke's behest.
- Mr Eric Jones, a chartered accountant who provided fake financial and other supporting information to assist with the completion of the mortgage application forms.

HCJ Ms Hudson, QC handed down the following sentences:

- White had pleaded guilty before the trial. The judge said that White had played a vital role in carrying out some key practical tasks of the fraud but was not a ringleader and had suffered much coercion over the years both to himself and his elderly mother. He had had the good sense to plead at the earliest opportunity and had demonstrated a real desire to repair the damage done by giving evidence to the Crown, and it was important evidence. Nevertheless, because of his expertise (knowledge of the banking business was at the heart of this fraud), he had known that what he was doing was illegal yet carried on doing it in return for substantial financial rewards. Therefore the sentence imposed by this court was **five** and a half years' imprisonment for fraud, obtaining money transfer by deception and subsequent money laundering of the profits, together with £10,000 defence costs.

- Banks had also pleaded guilty before the trial. The judge noted that she was full of remorse for her involvement in the crimes before this court, but accepted she was probably not aware that many of the management instructions she was directed to carry out were unlawful. However, ignorance of the law is no excuse, so she was sentenced to **three** years for assisting in obtaining money transfers by deception. However, the court was minded to suspend this sentence for three years given her current state of ill health in the USA. Defence costs are initially set at £5,000.

- John Stoddard and Eric Jones had both pleaded guilty before the trial for their roles in the fraud. The judge accepted that they were the "workers at the coalface not the organisers" but nevertheless they must have known that forging and falsifying documents etc. was against the law, so: "I sentence you to each serve **three** years in prison, and each to pay £5,000 defence costs."

- Thomas Brown had also pleaded guilty before the trial had commenced. The judge said, "You played a major day to day role in ensuring the fraud continued to operate successfully by completing the mortgage transactions. Although I am satisfied that you were not a ringleader as such, you also have abused your professional body and must have known that what you were doing was against the law but nevertheless continued to do it over a very long period of time. Therefore I sentence you to **four** years in jail, and order you to pay £10,000 defence costs."

Turning to the three defendants found guilty at the trial:

- Clarke was one of the three ringleaders of the operation, being the principal organiser on the ground of the necessary paperwork (principally delegated down to Messrs White and Brown). The judge said, "You knew what you were getting into, and used your position at Gouldings (a long-established and hitherto perfectly respectable family firm of solicitors) to breach the trust put in you by others. Your expertise and knowledge of the mortgage application process lay at the heart of this fraud and you abused the trust of the public and your professional body. Accordingly, this court sentences you to a minimum of **eight** years' imprisonment, and orders you to pay £25,000 towards defence costs."

- The Downing and Williamson sentencings were dealt with together. Having been found guilty of being the two main ringleaders of the whole operation, Judge Hudson said, "In all my years in the judiciary service I have never come across a case of a fraud network operated on such a massive scale that I have found in this case. You both used your positions in society to breach the trust imposed in you by others. You were, and still are, totally indifferent to the suffering caused to others involved. Your dishonesty, conceit and arrogance have blinded you to the consequences of your actions and, moreover, you had no compunction to abuse your positions in society for your own selfish and greedy ends. You would leave no stone unturned to get what you wanted, when you wanted it, whatever the cost to life. You abused the trust of the public and used your skilful professional laundering techniques to allow large sums of money to be 'syphoned off' for your own use, knowing that it was derived from the processes of criminal activity. This is a classic way of laundering and you must have known that, yet you were prepared to continue with these methods for many years. These sentences are not just to punish you but to act as a deterrent to anyone else tempted to act similarly. Therefore, the sentence of this court is that you should each go to jail for a minimum of **ten** years, and pay £50,000 defence costs."

An SFO case controller said, "This outcome demonstrates the effectiveness of combining the skills and expertise of SFO investigators, the CPS, lawyers and police forces nationally and internationally in bringing fraudsters to account.

I consider that it is a satisfactory result for the criminal justice system." He added, "Further legal action by the banks and mortgage lenders subject to the fraudulent activity exposed in this case is likely to follow.

I also would like to register special thanks to all of the authorities in the USA who have inputted in a major way to these successful convictions."

EPILOGUE 2

It was reported in the national press on 25 January 1994 that Steven Martin Johns had been granted a full pardon for the murder of Jon Armstrong in September1978.

Two men (not yet formally named but rumoured to be Messrs G. Williamson and R. H. Clarke) are currently being held at Her Majesty's pleasure for recent mortgage fraud, money laundering and other associated crimes and are expected to be charged with the murder of the aforementioned Jon Armstrong, together with the murder of Adam Best and the attempted murder of Ms Penelope Banks, imminently. There is a warrant out for the arrest of a third individual (a woman whose name has also not yet been released by the authorities but rumoured to be a Mrs V. Downing), who was also convicted for mortgage fraud, money laundering and other associated offences in the above-mentioned case but has recently escaped police custody and is currently on the run.

Any trial date arising out of these charges and arrest warrant has yet to be confirmed but it is anticipated that it will be within the next six to nine months.

EPILOGUE

Notwithstanding this recent announcement granting him a full pardon (thus confirming his innocence at long last), Steve had come to the conclusion that all he wished to do with his life now was to live in Florida and look after his new-found (albeit now disabled) cousin – nothing at all to keep him in GB, that's for certain. As far as he was concerned, he had no family in England anymore; Uncle Reg, you can go to hell.

Once there, he thought he might start to do some sea fishing – might take his mind off some of the events of the last 12 months. Surprisingly, after a short while, he had to begrudgingly admit to himself that it had gradually done the trick and had accordingly started to enjoy life again. "Why hadn't I tried this years ago?" he mused.

Then one day, whilst fishing off Naples Pier, he started chatting to another fisherman, who turned out to be a local guy who didn't appear to have two pennies to rub together but nevertheless soon discovered that he had been fishing there all his life! Just shows you, he thought, they say the best things in life are free (you try all your life to earn enough to realise your dream and retire to some island paradise only to find that when, for the lucky few, the dream actually turns into reality; there is this chap who has not had the pressures and stress of all that modern-day living but had been doing just that very thing all the time!). Seemed to him even more ironic when his thought process recalled JA's ultimate ambition in life when he retired (ie to sit off a pier fishing and smoking his favourite brand of cigars – if only he had done that from the off then perhaps none of this would ever have happened).

Then the clock struck one – time for some lunch, he thought: barbecued fish, just for a change (but oh how he missed Chris). He walked back to Penny in her wheelchair and found her asleep underneath her sun shade so he quietly released the brake and sidled off into the late afternoon sunshine, fishing rod (and catch) slung over his left shoulder.

At that precise moment, Reg was also sitting down to an evening meal of fish. He, though, was on his own (albeit racked with guilt as far as his nephew and daughter were concerned). Mainly, however, his thoughts were of Chris, whose funeral he had just returned from attending.

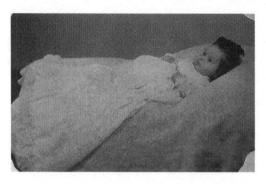

ABOUT THE AUTHOR

Conceived in Plymouth and born in Worcester but of Yorkshire parentage dating back to the early eighteenth century, I was a resident of north Staffordshire in my formative years but "returned home" after I got married and have since lived and worked in South Yorkshire. I have three grown-up daughters and four grandchildren.

Having studied locally (grammar school and FE college), I retired from a long career as a chartered surveyor in local government over a decade ago, but continued working part-time for a spell in various private-sector and agency roles "to keep my hand in"!

All of my past career roles involved substantial knowledge of the English property market.

My hobbies include: ornithology, swimming (still a few times a week), travelling (both home – especially the Orkney Islands, and Cornwall – and abroad, especially Lesvos and Tenerife), observing civil aircraft, football (mainly in the form of watching as many of Stoke City FC's teams as time allows) and, of course, genealogy.

The Ring's List is my inaugural novel.